The Evolution of Darwinism

the evolution of darwinism
study
•
k usha
•
first edition
august   2019
•
published
chintha publishers, thiruvananthapuram
•
typesetting
star communications, thiruvananthapuram
•
cover
vinod mangoes

Distribution
DESHABHIMANI BOOKHOUSE
H O Thiruvananthapuram 695035
Email: chinthapublishers@gmail.com
Website: www.chinthapublishers.com

Branch

Head Office Kunnukuzhi • Statue Thiruvananthapuram • KSRTC Bus Station Alappuzha • KSRTC Bus Station Ernakulam • Machingal Lane Thrissur • IG Road Kozhikode • Mavoor Road Kozhikode • NGO Union Building Kannur • Central Bus Terminal Complex Thavakkara Kannur

---

CO - 2841 / 5107
ISBN -978-93-89410-03-7

The Evolution of Darwinism

K Usha

CHINTHA PUBLISHERS
Thiruvananthapuram 695 035

K Usha

Belongs to Iritty in Kannur District. Now residing at Pazhassy in Mattannur. Retired from services as Headmistress in Sivapuram High School. Chintha has already published *Mahasasthra Prathibhakal Part II, Darwin paranjathum Darwin ariyathirunnathum under* Vijnanavarsham series.

Hai! Enthu Maduram, Minnaminugukal, Koodum Kadum, Irumbum Thurumbu, Kokkumanushian, Sharkkarapayasam, Enguninno vanna Thumbi, Nalla changathimar are other publications.

Husband   :   A P Prabhakaran (Resource Person)
(Mathematics)
Children   :   Syam, Sandeep, Sandhya
Address   :   Prathibha,
Pazhassy, Uruvuchal P O
Mattannor, Kannoor Dist.

CONTENT

PUBLISHERS NOTE

Darwin through his Evolution of species by natural selection presented revolutionary ideas about emergence of humanity. People of later generation used Darwinism intentionally to inculcate some false beliefs in capitalist society. This was based on struggle for existence and survival of fittest. This is against the vision that everyone has right to lead a decent life.

Mrs. Usha is particular that one should necessarily be conscious about the capitalist aberrations to Darwinism while recognizing the theory.

Chintha Publishers

1
Where Did you come from?

The most striking feature of the living world is its variety. We widely divde the living world into plants and animals. But we know that all plants are not alike. There are single celled plants that can be watched only with the help of a microscope. The giant sequoa trees also belong to the plant kingdom. Among plants the characteristics like the seent, colour and shape of leaves and flowers and the size of the fruits vary from plant to plant. The morphological characters are also different. There are herb, shrubs, creepers and trees. There are acquatic plants as well as terrestrial. When we come to the animal world the variety is more fascinating. Both Blue whale and Amoeba are the subjects of animal kingdom. Take a single character for example namely movement. Some of animals swim, some float, some walk, some hop and some jump. Some walk on four legs, Some walk on thousand legs, yet some of them are legless. Then of course there are human beings walking on two legs.

It is estimated that there are about 10 million types of plants and animals on earth. Nobody can give the exact number because every year some new plants and animals are discovered somewhere in the world and some plants and animals extinct in another corner.

As a result of Hybridisation grafting, budding and tissue culture man develops new varieties of plants and animals.

How all these living things came to being? Has somebody created them independently? These questions puzzled man from time immemorial. Now even a primary school kid knows their answers. Life first appeared in water as minute acellular organisms. They gradually evolved into the wonderful living organisms that we find around us. Now organic evolution is considered as a very important branch of life science.

Then, what is evolution? It is change. J B S Haldane, the well known Biologist define evolution as a change that occurs very slowly. But, apart from change it is a development towards a higher plane. In the prehistoric period all the living beings on earth were of simple structure. They underwent gradual change and modification to become the plants and animals with very complicated structure as we see now.

In the earlier days people belived that all living organisms were created by a master Architect. Religions called this creator, God. Everything was created as we see them now. This is the theory of creation. Each religion has their own Gods and their own stories of creation.

According to Hinduism the God in charge of creation is Brahma. In Holy Bible, the book of Genesis puts forward the exact time table of creation. On the first day God created light. Second day he created sky. See, earth and plants were created on the third day. On the fourth day the creation of Sun, moon and starts took place. The question can there be plants before the creation of Sun is irrelevent. The next day, that is on the fifth day all the aquatic animals and birds were created. Terrestrial animals and human beings were created on the sixth day. After the six consecutive days of creation on the seventh day God took rest. The other religions also have their own version of creation.

Even in the olden times there were a few who rejected these

stories of creation. In ancient India there was a belief that every organism consisted of minute particles called 'Kanas.' The sages who advocated this theory were called 'Kanadas.' There was another Indian belief that living bodies are made of five objects. These were water, earth, air, sky and fire. Indians call them 'Pancha bhuthas'.

Thales, the famous Greek Philosopher and Mathematician believed that life originated from water. But Anaksimenus, one of his contomporaries argued that life was originated from air and water vapour. Empidoelis, another Greek thinker said that it was from a combination of earth, air, water and fire life was originated. However, in Grece there was general belief that Sun was very important for all living things.

Aristotle was the deciple of great Plato. Aristotle is considered as the father of scientific method. Reasoning is the basis of science. We owe to Aristotle for developing scientific thought and reasoning. It was he who started the method of classifying plants and animals according to their salient features. Still he believed that fish were generated from mud and worms germinate from decaying flesh. What an irony!

By fifth century A D christianity became very powerful and influential in Europe. The theory of creation again occupied the centre stage. The church and clergy decided what was to be learned and what was to be discussed. Anybody who put forward ideas against religious belief was led to inquisition courts. But history teaches us that no permanent barrior could be raised before englightened minds. In 1543 Copernicus declared that sun is the centre of Universe against the popular belief that everything is placed around earth. Next is was the turn of Galileo. He shook the eitadels of religion by telling the world what he saw through his telescope. Of course the clergy imprisoned him. But prison walls could not keep his ideas in darkness.

Galileo died in 1642. Isaac Newton was born in the next year. Newton put forward the law of gravitation and three laws of motion.

These laws helped to explain the physical forces that govern natural phenomena. Newton's laws persuaded naturalists to watch organic evolution also as a natural phenomenon.

By seventeenth century science began to change the world. But there were many who firmly believed in the theory of creation of course, the theologists led this bandwagon. In 1620 Bishop Light foot made a very interesting revelation. He declared God created Adam, the first man on 21 October 4004 B C. It should be noted that this man was the chancellor of Cambridge University when he made this wonderful discovery. Geroge Cuvier, another well known naturalist came forward with a theory, that he called 'Theory of catastrophe'. According to this theory natural disasters like earthquake, volcanic eruption and flood cause the complete destruction of living organisms in a particular area. Then organisms from other parts of the world immigrate to that vacant land and these immigrants start to live as new species. Cuvier believed the fossils were the remainings of the extincts animals. Karl Linnaus who classified plants and animals and gave them scientific names (Binommeal nomanclature) firmly believed that each animal and plant was created seperately.

French Revolution that took place in 1789 brought about drastic changes in political, social economic and cultural fields in whole Europe. The first revolutionary idea on evolution also came from France.

Newton's laws inspired Comte de Buffon, the renowned French naturalist who put forward the idea that living organisms originated from some common ancestor.

The similarities between some animals and plants led him to this idea. We pointed out the similarities between man and monkey and argued that they were deseended from a common ancestor. He believed that the domesticated animals would find their wild relatives in the forests. But his christian belief was stronger than his scientific curiosity. He knew that it was dangerous to say anything against the theory of creation. So he presented his own theories as more probabilities or speculation. Still, his ideas were so original that he is considered as the father of Theory of Evolution.

But his most important contribution to scientific world is not this theory, but the famous naturalist Jean Baptiste Lamarck. Who was Lamarck? Let's find out.

2
Lamarck and Giraffes

Lamarck was the first scientist who declared that evolution obeyed certain natural laws. He was born on Ist August 1744 in Picardy in France. He was the youngest son of a poor but aristocratic family. Almost all the male members of his family served in military. As a boy Lamarck also wanted to become a soldier. But his father wanted him to join the college and graduate.

Lamarck continued his studies till 1760. That year his father passed away. Immediately after his father's death he possessed a horse and set out to join the army. At that time French army was fighting against Prussia. The seventeen year old Lamarck directly went to the battle field.

The bravery and the determination of the young boy impressed every one. In the battle field itself he was promoted as an officer. His friends wanted to celebrate this. One of them took up young Lamarck in his hands and rotated him like a doll. Unfortunately this jubilation caused a very serious injury to his neck. He was sent to paris for treatment. He underwent a very complicated surgery. He was forced to remain in bed for a year. He had to live on an annual pension of 400 francs. He sought some other profession. At first he joined a medical school hoping to become a doctor. But he had to give up it because of bad health. Then he found out another Teacher. He was famous French naturalist Bernad de Jussieu. Lamarck studied plant science from him.

For the next ten years Lamarck vividly studied about the different varieties of plants in France and published a book on it. Buffon happened to read this book and helped Lamarck to get a membership of 'French Academy of Sciences.'

Between 1781 and 83 Lamarck visited various museums and Botanical gardens in Europe. He collected rare plants that were not available in the royal garden and also other objects of natural history such as minerals and ores that were not found in French museums. In 1788 Lamarck was appointed as the keeper of the herbarium of Royal Garden with a yearly salary of 1000 francs.

It is said that in 1790 at the height of the French Revolution Lamarck changed the name of the Royal Garden from 'Jardin du Roi' to 'Jardin de plantes.' This name did not imply such a close association with French Royal family so that the revolutionary army spared it. After five years Lamarck was promoted as the curator of Natural History Museum in Paris.

Like most of his contemporaries Lamarck also believed in the theory of special creation. But the fossils exhibited in the museum forced him to think in another way. He began to believe that fossils are evidence of extinct animals because they were different from the animals that he saw around. What caused their destruction? Was it that the creator himself destroyed them? Lamarck put forward his ideas in a reserach paper published in 1802.

Lamarck believed that animals were not destroyed but they undergo gradual change from one form to another. In the begining there were only plants and animals with simple structure. Lamarck argued that organisms moved from simple to complex in a steady predictable way based on certain fundamental physical principles.

There he faced another questions. What caused such a change in living organisms? Lamarck stated that the enviornment in which an organism lived played a crucial role in causing such changes.

Lamarck employed several mechanisms as drivers of evolution, drawn from the common knowledge of his day and from his own belief in chemistry. He used these mechanisms to explain the two forces he saw as the causes of evolution. The first one was a force driving animals from simple to complex forms and the second one a force that helped them to adapt to their local environments and differentiating them from each other. So we can define evolution based on certain physical theories. In this way Jean Baptiste Lamarck rejected the presence of a divine hand behind the creation of living world.

How did the changes in the enviornment cause changes in the living organisms? Lamarck explained it in this way. Some environmental changes force them more frequent and continuous use of some organs. These organs gradually strengthens, develops and enlarges and slowly transformed into a new organ; while permanent disuse of any organ weakens and deterorates it and progressively diminishes its functional capacity until it finally disappears. These changes are transferred to the next generation. After three or four generations the offsprings will be entirely different from its ancestors. A very nice idea. Isn't it?

What effected such changes in living organisms? Here also Lamarck had his own explanations. The flow of certain liquids inside the living body effected the growth or diminishing of a certain organ in animals. Suppose an animal is in need of the enlargement of a particular organ. These vital fluids in flow towards that organ in large quantity. That results an extra growth to that part of the body. When an organ is not in use for a long period the vital fluid from that part is withdrawn towards the interior of the body. One thing should be specially noted here. Lamarck lived in an age of modern chemistry.

Still he favoured the then more traditional theory based on the classical four elements that is "air, earth, fire and water." During his lifetime Lamarck became controversial, attacking the more enlightened chemistry proposed by Lavoisier who is considered as the father of modern chemistry.

Lamarck proposed his theories in a quite scientific way citing several examples. We know that burrowing animals usually have no eyes and birds have no teeth. Lamarck argued that these changes are because of disuse. The classic example put forward by him is the neck of Giraffe and legs of snakes.

According to Lamarck the ancestors of Giraffes had normal neck. Due to some unknown reason there had been a shortage of food matierals on the ground. They had to raise their necks to eat leaves from the branches. Their necks began to elongate due to continuous use. This change was preserved and passed to the new individuals they produced, provided that the acquired modifications are there in both sexes. After a few generations the giraffes with long neck that now we see appeared. The state of snakes is the other way round. The ancesstors of snakes did have legs. But because of their life style they moved on their belly. Continuous disuse led to the disapperance of their legs!

Lamarckian principles are generally known as use and disuse theory or the inheritance of acquired characters. In fact this theories originated at time when scientists had no idea how herditory characters are transferred over generations. Now even a common man knows that acquired modifications are never inherited. There are historical evidences to prove it.

From prehistoric time people used to pierce their ears and noses to accommodate ornaments. In earlier days both men and women did this. Even now we know that this habit is not fully eradicated. Yet no infant is born with holes on its nose or ear. This shows that young ones do not inherit the acquired modification of their parents physical nature. In ancient China it was believed that beautiful women should have small feet. So immediately after birth the infant girls feet were bandaged very tightly. Parents brutally folded their little toes backward to make the feet look smaller. Generation after generation they did this stubburnly as a ritual. Yet the girls were born with normal feet.

It took many years for scientists to discover the mechanism of inheritance. Despite his principles Lamarck believed that minute organisms are created by spontaneous generation and simple organisms thus created being transmuted over time becoming more complex. At his time Lamarck was criticised not because of his principles of inheritance, but for not believing in the theory of creation. He came into conflict with widely respected palaentologist Geroge cuvier, who was not a supporter of evolution. Naturalists, under the leadership of Cuvier attacked his theories severely. They are afraid that if scientific world recognized the gradual transformation of livingbeings the theory of direct creation would become irrelevant.

Although Lamarck was not the first thinker to advocate organic evolution he was the first to develop a truly coherent evolutionary theory. Lamarck gradually turned blind and died in Paris on December 18, 1829. When he died his family of so poor that they had to apply to the Academic for financial assistance for his funeral. Lamarck's books and the articles of his home were sold at auction and his body was buried in a temporary lime pit. In his obituary also George Cuvier ridiculed Lamarck. But we should remember one thing. The only evolutionary theory existed in Europe at time of Darwin was Lamarck's principle of inheritence of acquired characters. Though his proposed mechanism of evolution was gradually rejected Lamarck's seven volume work on the natural history of invertibrates is recognised as a lasting contribution to Zoology.

Before coming to Darwin I have to mention one more name.

That is Robert Chambers. His field of interest was not Zoology, but Geology. He argued that when God decides that there should be a new variety of animals on earth, on of the existing animal gives birth to a new offspring. According to him the changes occur at the time of development of the embryo. God effects these changes. No scientific evidence or proofs. But it was only Chamber's hypothesis. These new offsprings will be quite different from their parents.

Robert Chambers explained that three strange offsprings move up the ladder of evolution from simple to complicated. No doubt, everything was according to the will of God. Still he published his book anonimously, fearing the wrath of Cuvier and company. This book fascinated Victorian readers very much and it had twelve editions. The book *Vestiges of Natural history of creation* has only a historical value, because it was the only book on Evolution widely read before Darwin.

3

Darwin Starts his Voyage

Charles Robert Darwin was born on February 12, 1809 at the house called 'The Mount' in Shrewburg, Shorpshire, England. His father Robert Darwin and grandfather Erasmus Darwin were doctors. His mother's name was Susannah. Robert and Susannah Darwin had six children. Charles was the second youngest. His family affectionately called him Bobby or Charley. The Darwins' was a very rich family.

It was the onset of Industrial Revolution. Several factories were built in and around the great city of England. The newly established railway helped people from distant villages to come to the city seeking factory jobs. Queen Victoria's ships explored unknown waters and anchored at distant ports. They brought back rawmaterials for the industries and found out new markets for their products.

At the sametime the great Universities of England like Oxford and Cambridge were under the control of church. Any thought against church and religion was nipped in bud. The French revolution which happened in 1789 had already terrified political and religious leaderships. However hard the authorities concerned tried they could not prevent the ideas of liberty, equality and democracy from entering the atmosphere of England. At the same time the Sailors who visited distant countries brought news about the people and wonderful things they saw there.

The navigators brought home some wonderful collections of fossils and rocks. Paleantologists and Geologists had a great occasstion for study and research. Some scientists firmly declared that the earth was much older than Bishop Lightfoot calculated. The fossils made naturalists like Lamarck to think about evolution that we have seen in the previous chapter. The people who travelled around the world taled about human beings they found there. The colour and physical structure of men and women they met in Africa, India, West Indies and Australia were quite different from that of Europeans. They were sure that if God had created men in His own shape there would not be such difference. All these ideas excited the English scientific world. It was at this time little Charlie started his education.

Robert Darwin was a man with progressive outlook. He had no deep faith in reglion or God. He always encouraged new thoughts and ideas. Being himself a doctor he wanted his eleder son Erasmus and younger son Charlie to become doctors.

As a little boy Charlie was very fond of the world outside their house. He loved going for long walk along the banks of the river Severn. He enjoyed climbing the trees in the orchard beside their house and stuffing himself with fruits. It was more enjoyable because those trees were not owned by his family and he was not supposed to pluck fruits from them.

Nature facinated little Darwin very much. He longed to travel and see all the wonderful sights. He had a habit of collecting anything he could lay his hands on. The boy's collection included plants, stones and insects.

When Darwin was about eight years his mother died. But little Charlie did not have to bear the brunt of that tragedy as his elder sisters took over the task of caring the yonger children. First Darwin went to a local school. It was run by one Mr. Case. Later he alongwith his elder brother Erasmus joined a school run by a priest called Rev. Samuel Butler. He had to learn Greek and Latin at Butler's school. He didn't like both. But Chemistry fascinated him. His brother set up a Chemistry laboratory at their home. He kindly allowed Charlie to assist him in the lab. He read a lot of books on Chemistry at that time. Some of their experiments were mysterious and it produced gases with foul smell. Because of this Darwin's friends nicknamed him as gas. His sisters feared that one day they would blow off the house. When new about their experiments reached school Rev. Butler scolded them severely and advised not to waste their time on such futile things.

While studying in school, Darwin became an expert in using guns. But his interest in shooting birds soon gave way to bird watching. He observed the birds and prepared notes on their habitat and behaviour. Darwin spent seven years at school. But his grades were not satisfactory and he could not impress his teachers with any special talent. His elder brother was very studious and joined the Cambridge University to study medicine. Now Charlie had to go to school alone. It was unbearable for him. He spent his time playing with dogs, watching birds and catching rats. Robert Darwin was very much warried about his spoilt son. "You are a disgrace to this family" His father used to tell him. "What do you know otherthan hunting birds and playing with dogs?" How could he know that his youngest son was destined to restructure the mindset of a generation.!

When Darwin was sixteen his father wanted him to help him with his medical practice. Darwin liked the job and when his father decided to send him to one of the best medical school at Edinburgh, Darwin didn't object to it. Since Erasmus had completed his course at Cambridge he also joined Charlie at Edin burgh. The brothers together took up a house and Charles Darwin started attending the medical school.

At that time sedatives were not known and doctors conducted surgeries without the help of anaesthesia. The howling patients were held firmly while the surgery was being done. Darwin could not stand at these scenes. The patients fainted from pain and Darwin almost fainted himself each time. He was convinced that this was not his profession.

At the medical school there were some subjects that Darwin liked very much. So he continued his medical education for some time. One of them was Chemistry. Pro. Thomas Hope was his Chemistry teacher. He was a brilliant teacher and Darwin enjoyed his classes very much. The second subject was Taxidermy; that is the science of preserving and stuffing animal skins. A man named John Edmonstone taught him that skill. Mr. Jhon Edmonstone was a blackman and had been a slave in Guyana South America. Mr. Edmonstone talked to Darwin for hours on end about South America. This conversation arose Darwin's imagination. He dreamed of exploring the mysterious dense forests of South America and imagined the strange animals and birds lived there. These wonderful daydreams helped him to escape from the boredom of medical studies.

Darwin got through the first year. During vaction he read a book about Natural History written by Mr. Gilbert White. That was a great work and it taught Darwin the importance of observing everything very closely and keeping detailed notes.

The holidays ended Darwin got back to Edinburgh. As Erasmus had moved back to London he felt lonely. He could not tolerate the medical classes so that he spent more time in the natural history museum. At that time in Edinburgh there was a small organisation called plinian society. The members of this society held regular meetings and discussed scientific topics. It was from these discussions Darwin got the idea that everything in the Bible need not to be taken as the literal truth. That was a bold new thought, because at that time for people like Darwin Bible was a very important part of their lives still he kept his idea as a secret.

At Edinburgh Darwin got a new friend. He was Robert Grant who was a Zoologist. It was from this friend Darwin heard the word organic evolution for the first time. Until then like any other Christian Darwin also believed that God created the animals and plants around him just as they were. Darwin and Robert Grant used to go on long walks and they discussed the various ideas of evolution. It was Mr. Grant who introduced Darwin to Lamarck's theory of use and disuse. Darwin found Lamarckian principles very interesting and he noted that they lack scientific evidence.

Among all these things Darwin neglected his medical studies and soon quit it. After that he went on a tour of Paris with his mother's brother Josaih Wedge Wood II. Darwin's father did not like the life his prodigal son was following. Robert Darwin was determined that Charlie should have some profession. So he enrolled Charles Darwin for a course of study which would qualify him to be a priest. Robert Darwin selected the famous Christ college at Cambridge University for his son. But the 'would be' priest was more interested in collecting beetlles than studying theology.

Around this time one of Darwin's cousins introduced him to Rev. Jhon Stevens Henslow. He was a professor of Botany at Cambridge. Darwin attended his classes regularly and was amazingly attracted towards him. Prof. Henslow also liked him very much. Soon he began to invite Darwin for dinner parties. These parties were get together of interesting people who discussed interesting subjects.

Rev. Henslow suggested several books for Darwin to read. Among them Preliminary Discourse on the study of Natural Philosophy fascinated him very much. This was written by a man named Sir Jhon Herschel. From this book Darwin understood there were myriad mysteries in nature waiting for him to be discovered by scientific investigation. He firmly decided that his fature career would be something related to natural science. But his father had sent him to Cambridge to become a priest. So Darwon completed his studies at christ college and passed his final examination in 1930. However he did not follow that profession.

Rev. Henslow knew Darwin's passion for nature well. So he

advised him to go for a study tour to somewhere in the tropics- So Darwin made a plan to visit canary islands. One of his friends Marmaduke Ramsay agreed to accompany him. As a preparation Darwin took a crash course under Prof. Sedgewick in Geology. This also was Prof. Henslow's suggestion. But all his preparations were in vain because of the sudden death of Ramsay. Darwin was disappointed. Again Prof. Henslow came to his aid.

British government decided send a ship, HMS Beagle on a very important voyage. That is to survey the coast of South America. The Captain of this ship wanted a naturalist as his assistant. The selected person should work hard and that also without any honorarium. Captain Fitzroy approached Prof. Henslow to findout such a person without a second thought. Henslow recommended Darwin's name.

When Darwin knew this his joy knew no limit. But it was not easy to convince his father. The father knew his son well. He never took his life seriously and this voyage also was on of his fancies. He was not going to allow his crazy son to leave home and stay on board for two years at least. His sisters also took his fathers side and Darwin was in dilemma. At last Darwin's uncle Josiah Wedgewood came out to help his nephew. He wrote to Darwin's father that this voyage was quite suitable to Darwin's character and aptitude. The trip would help him to sharpen his interests in natural science. In the end Darwin's father gave in. He also agreed to provide the money he needed.

Finally on the morning to December 27, 1831 HMS Beagli sailed out of Plymouth Harbour of England with Charles Robert Darwin on board with a mind brimming with dreams. The twenty two year old youngman who was destined to lead lifescience through a road untrodden till then said farewell to his fatherland with a heavy heart.

4
The origin of a book

This was Darwin's first voyage and seasickness made him uneasy. The sweet memories of the dear faces that were left behind increased his grief. To overcome these agony Darwin resorted to reading. He had taken with him a very interesting book. It was *The Principles of Geology* written by Charles Lyell.

Lyell strongly disagreed with the theory of catastrophe. Lyell argued that the earth had been experiencing a series of natural changes which build up overtime to big changes. Darwin liked this idea very much. Darwin found an evidence to prove this theory from the sandiago beach of south America. There he observed sea shells stuck on rocks about forty five meter high from sea level. How could they reach there? Ofcourse the sea level had come down over time. This can be taken as a proof that the earth's surface was undergoing gradual changes.

Wonders were waiting Darwin in the rain forests of Brazil. He saw insects and plants that he had never seen in England. He had enough training in collecting specimens and preserving them. This experience helped Darwin very much in South America. He sent all these specimens plants, rocks and stones to Prof. Henslow. Some of the bundles contained a fossils also. "Why" exclaimed captain Fitzroy "are you sending all these wastes to England?" Apart from strange animals Darwin met stange men and women in SouthAmerica. They were quite different from the people of Eurpoe. As a young naturalist this difference attracted Darwin's attention and confused him as well. He thought a lot about it.

On 31 September 1835 HMS Beagls set out to Galapagos island. That was the most important milestone of the journey. In the begining Darwin was not very excited because he did not know what was in store for him there. Darwin was wonder struck by the sight of the gigantic tortoises there. The mates of the ship caught some of them for meat. Darwin pilifered two of the animals and kept aside to send to his friends in England. Another species that arose his curiosity was birds. All the islands in the Galapagoes had plenty of birds, especially Finches. But in every island their morphological features and feeding habits were different. Darwin collected different varieties of Finches. There were iguanas also. Iguanas are reptiles similar to varanus and garden lizards Darwin found two types of Iguanas. One variety was land living animal that feed on plants. Another Variety could swim and fed on see-weed and algae. How could this variation occur to animals living in the same area very close together? His mind was full of such questions. But Darwin was too busy to sit up and think about thier answers. Sometimes some answers flashed in his brain. But they were contradictory to the theological lessons he had learnt.

The HMS Beagle continued its journey. Their next destination was Newzealand and then Australia. Here also Darwin found strange people and animals. Just imagine the expression of Charles Darwin when he first saw a Kangaroo hoping along the bushy land of Australia. At that time Australia and Newzealand were collectively called Antipodes. Had god created some special animals for the Antipodes? This thought amused Darwin. They visited Cocos Islands

Mauritius, Cape town, St. Helena and many other places. After going back to salvador to re-take some measurements. The HMS Beagle set course for England. On October 2, 1836. Their ship anchored at Falmouth. they had been away for four years, nine months and five days.

Darwin had matured verymuch and his family was happy to welcome his back. But his mind was full of the 'junk' he had sent home from various ports. What might have been Prof. Henslow and other naturalists doing with them? He was eager to know.

While Darwin was exploring the unknown world, here in England Prof. Henslow and his scientists friends were keenly examining the fossils and specimens Darwin sent. The new findings excited the scientific world. Darwin had collected Thirteen different types of Finches from Galapagos. Biologists came to the conclusion that all the Thirteen Finches belogned to Thirteen species. What does it mean by the word species? Species is the smallest unit of animal and plant classification. Members of a species are similar and can breed together to produce fertile young animals or plants. Despite the differences in the morphological features all human beings belong to a single species.

The fossils that Darwin sent from South America facinated naturalists. The fossils had similarities with the animals that lived in that place. But they were not same. There were several differences between the then living animals and the fossils. The naturalists of England soon recognized Darwin as one among them. But Darwin knew well that he had presented only some conclusions and vague ideas. He had to work hard to get them recognised as scientific principles. He dedicated the next two decades of his life for this purpose.

The idea of organic evolution first came to Darwin's mind while watching the Finches of Galapagos. He found that Finches of Galapagos islands were quite different from that of South America.

At the Same time they had striking similarities also. So Darwin began to think that all these birds were deseended from a common ancestor. This conclusion would be applicable to other animals as well. Living beings experience continuous changes, during their lifetime. Some of these changes are inherited by next generation. After a few generations the inherited characters make them a new species. If that was the case, all living things should have a common ancestor. Then what about man? Darwin had no doubt. All human beings were descended from a common ancestor.

That was a brilliant idea. But in the victorian society nobody would accept if. People believed that human beings were a special creation of God. There were people who believed the black people were inferior to white skinned people and even women got inferior postion than men. If all individuals black or white, men or women were descended from a common ancestor every one should get equal importance, at least in the view point of science. Darwin knew that the victorian society would not forgive him. He could make them recognise his ideas only if he could put forward strong, undeniable evidence. Darwin shared his ideas only with a few very close friends.

Darwin wrote a few articles and books on his voyage. He made talks on subjects like geological changes structure of coral reefs, outlandish animals and birds, strange men and women that he met on the far off lands. In 1938 Darwin happened to read an essay by Rev. Malthus on population.

Rev. T R Malthus was an economist employed in the East India company. Malthus wrote about the danger of huge population growth. The industrial revolution attracted a large number of people from different parts of British Islands to London, seeking jobs. The population in the city increased but the resources like food materials and housing facilities did not increase at that rate. There happened a competition for resources. According to Malthus in this competition the weak were eliminated and only strong survived. People who developed special skills were able to fit themselves to the situation and therefore increased their chances in life. In fact Rev. Malthus had no sympathy towards the poor. He even argued that their elimination was necessary for the progress and prosperity of the nation. According to him the population explosion could be controlled by shipping the poor people to Australia.

Darwin was not as hard hearted as Malthus. So his theories did not attract Darwin. But the idea of 'Survival of the fittest' fascinated him. He began to think about it again and again. He began to feel that all life was something like Malthus describd. There were always more livingthings born than could be survived with the given resources. So there must be competition among them. Only those who better adapted to face the competition survived. Only better equipped ones could produce offsprings. These offspring could adjust with their surroundings better than their parents. Gradually they evolve into new species.

In his autobiography Darwin admits that Malthus had influenced him. But it was not Malthus who inspired Darwin to think about organic evolution as some people claim. Darwin was a brilliant explorer and committed researcher. He had remarkable power of reasoning. All these combined together to form his favourite idea of organic evolution. By 1938 Darwin had formed this idea with mathematical precision. But he started writing only in 1942. So we can't underestimate Darwin's genius and give unnecessary credit to Rev. Malthus. At first Darwin wrote an essay about 35 pages. Later he expanded it as a book with 270 pages. Still he hesitated to send it to his publishers. Charles Lyell, Darwin's friend and adviser insisted him on sending the completed work to the publisher. At this time something interesting happened.

Darwin came acoross a research paper written by a young naturalist Alfred Russel wallace. Wallace was exploring the Malay Archipelago. Wallace himself sent the paper to Darwin with a request to go through it and give an opinion. Wallace also was interested in the formation of species. In his paper Wallace wrote about how variations or changes lead to the formation of new species. Darwin was shocked to read the paper because the conclusion of that young naturalist was very close to Darwin's idea of organic evolution. This strange coincidence puzzled Darwin.

He read it again and again with great relief Darwin found out that Wallace's theory differed a lot from his own. Wallace believed that the final goal of evolution is man. Evolution would make man a better more moral and more rational and more perfect being. But Darwin didn't believe in any such goal of evolution. He argued that the changes are random and the variations that survived purely depended on the environment. Wallace believed the process of evolution was controlled by a supreme power. But Darwin argued that variations take place according to certain natural laws cooperation between animals led to evolution. This was wallace's view. Darwin explained the other way round. He said that struggle for existance between individuals and varieties of the same species resulted in evolution. Despite these difference the essence of the two papers was same.

All this happened in 1858. Darwin was forced to publish his book along with Wallace's paper. Extracts from Darwin's book and part of Wallace's work on species were read out to the Linnean Society, London on July 1, 1958. The audience heard it out in silence but most of them were not ready to believe it. The scientific world of London was also not much excited. Darwin returned to the finishing work of his book on November 24, 1859 Darwin's book *Origin of species by Natural selection* Published 1250 copies were printed and most of them were sold out on that day itself. January 7, 1860 its second edition was on sale. This time 3000 copies were printed. Till 1876 sixeen Thousand copies of Darwin's book were sold in England. It was a record sale as far as a scientific work was concerned. *Origin of species* was translated into most of the European languages including Russian. In his autobiography Darwin wrote that an article was published in Hebrew language saying that there was nothing new in Darwin's book. The author claimed that all the points Darwin presented in his book were already started in old Testament. Darwin also says that more than two hundred articles and some books were written criticising *origin of species*. Even now Darwin and Darwinism are favourite subjects of authors.

Darwin presented some revolutionary ideas through this book. What were these ideas; why they were called revolutionary, Let's have a look into it.

5
Wonderful variations

In 1859, when Darwin published *origin of species* the area of Biological ignorance was very large as Julian Huxley stated, Darwin knew nothing of the laws that defined the transfer of hereditory traits from parents to offsprings. Darwin confesses this ignorance in his work. Georgor Mendel, an Austrian priest had already discovered the law of heredity. Unfortunately the scientific world was unaware of it at that time. We can go through the details of that discovery later. Now we can follow Charles Darwin.

In the opening chapter Darwin tells about domestication of birds and animals. According to him climate, feeding habits and circumstances are the main causes of variation in plants and animals. At the sametime variations are seen between plants that grow from the seeds of the same fruit. Similarly strong differences appear in the young ones of the same litter. Sometimes young ones show similarity to some remote ancestor. So he begins to think that there are same natural laws that govern heredity, growth and reproduction. As stated earlier he was totally ignorant of the laws controlling heredity. But all the same features found both in parents and offsprings cannot be attributed to heredity. Because, all these animals live in same environment. But Darwin points out some features which can be called heredity without any doubt.

The absence of melanin pigments makes one's skin and hair very white and eyes pink. This condition is knows as albinism. In same families this condition is found genetically transferred from parents to offsprings. If a defect like albinism can be transferred gentically can't all physical features be transferred from one generation to next. Darwin reasoned that a person's morphological characters are mainly based on his or her heredity.

Another interesting fact Darwin noted is that our domesticated animals have more variants than their wild relatives living in the forests. Our domestic dogs and wolves are closely related. But the variants that we see among domestic dogs are not there among the wild wolves. There are different types of domesticated dogs like Greybhound, blood hound, terrier, spaniel and bulldog. Darwin was confident that strong evidence are there that all these variants are descended from a single wild stock. Also this will be an answer to the arguments that all speicies remain unchanged since their creation. Some people believed that each domestic animal was descended from a seperate ancestor. If that was right we had to believe that in Europe there had been at least twenty different varieties of wild cows and goats. Darwin's common sense did not allow him to admit this. To collect more evidence he decided to make a special study on domestic pigeons.

Darwin's study on pigeons was total and complete. He associated himself with several pigeon Ganciers and joined two of the London pigeon clubs. He purchased on obtained every breed he could. His friends from different parts of the world especially India and Persia sent stuffed pigeon skins. He read articles published on pigeons in different langauges. Finally he was able to talk about pigeon as an authority.

The diversity of the breeds astonished Darwin. His scientific study helped him to reach the conclusion that all domestic pigeons are originated from a wild variety named 'Columba Livia.' At first pigeon breeders laughed at him. Bud Darwin proved that all these variants could interbreed and produce fertile offsprings.

How different types of variants appear among domestic animals, In some species special features appear all on a sudden. Darwin noted that in most cases these modifications are found beneficiary to breeders rather than the breeds. So farmers intentionally select animals with favourable variations to breed. This selection is conducted generation after generation. During this process the smaller variations are accumulated and become larger variations. The plants and animals that we now see are the product of continuous selection that occured through hundreds of years.

Men resorted to selection process to produce improved varieties of plants and animals. Even in ancient societies there existed some methods of selection. Darwin collected enough evidences to prove this. In England there were laws preventing the exports of somekinds of animals on the other hand government encouraged the import of some kind of plants and animals. From prehistoric time farmers removed plants and animals with unfavourable variations from their farm land. During the time of famine or flood farmers protect there favourite domestic animals and others were neglected. The protected animals got more chances for reproduction. The others were perished. So we can say that the animals and plants that we see around us now are the result of careful selection and breeding that happened through centuries. To find out their ancestors is not a easy task because the variation had made them entirely different.

Now come to Nature. During the last few centuries man developed thousands of new varieties of plants and animals, through the process of selection. Then why should we hesitate to believe that all the living things on earth are selected and protected by Nature through a period of 3000 million years. Then Darwin explains how variations occured to plants and animals in Nature.

All individuals of one species are not alike. There are slight individual differences. These differences, even though they may be very small are very important. As stated earlier they accumulate to form larger variations. Even naturalists find it very difficult to identify all the variants of a particular species. One scientist may consider all variants as one species. But another may mark them as different species. At the time of classification most scientists neglect these variations and may consider them as one species. Darwin thought the varieties which were more distinct and permanent as steps towards more strongly marked and permanent varieties. The latter leads to subspecies and then to new species. Darwin stated that minute morphological modifications accumulated by natural selection leads to the formation of a new species. So all the different variants can be seen as the archaic form of a species. At the same time all the achaic terms do not transform into species. Some archaic forms themselves become extinct. Some remain as such for a long period of time. The species dwelling in wide area and having more number exhibit more variations than speices living in limited area with less numbers. The diverse physical circumstances and competiton with other living organisms might be reasons for this.

Suppose, a certain species are seen abundand in a particular area. What does it mean. No doubt, there will be some favourable conditions for that species in that area. Similarly if large scale variations occur to a certain species in any particular area we can guess that there must be some conditions favouring variations in that area.

Some species flourish in number in a certain area at some point of time. But they need not remain in that state for ever. The species once flurished and dominated over others, later come down in number and reach the verge of extinction. The changes in their environment effects this kind of perishing of some species.

Darwin made these observations about one fifty years ago. Now-a-days we hear a lot about plants and animals become extinct. We learn about endangered species now face extinction. We have prepared 'Red Data Book' to list them. The changes in the environment like pollution causes variation in different species. These variations or modifications help them overcome the unfavourable condition, that is pollution. Some of these variations might evolve into dangerous species. We are now previously facing a situation, where bacteria becoming resistant to antibodies and pests becoming resistant to commonly used pesticides.

Species and their variations an distinguished from one another based on the differences. When the difference is very minute it is called a variation. If the difference are very remarkable then they are called species. Genus is a group which include more than one species. Species comming under a genus will be similar in many ways. The difference between two species under a genus can be compared to the difference between two variations of a species.

Darwin made some wonderful studies on adaptation in animals and birds. Adaptation is a change in morphology or behaviour in order to be successful in a new situation. When we look around we can see several adaptations. These adaptations help them lead a better life in a particular enviornment. The feet of wood pecker, the bugs that live between the feathers of birds and winged seeds that are flown along with the wind are amazing examples of adaptation.

The enigmatic transformation of variations into species raises several questions. How are the genuses formed? will adaptations lead to formation of species and genus? Charles Darwin stands before us with his famous answer, that is 'struggle for existence.'

$$\textbf{6}$$

Natural Selection

All living being engage in competition with others for their existence. Darwin was not the first man to put forward this idea. Several Philosophers had already stated this. We have seen how Darwin got this idea from Malthusian essay. With this idea in mind Darwin began to watch the nature very closely. Behind its beautiful and attractive face, the Nature hides its greater tendency for competition and annihilation. The same bird that fills the air with sweet music, kills and eats worms and butterflies. The birds which eatup seeds of plants and beatles have their own security problems. Animals like snakes and cats feed upon their eggs and little ones. The living being produce offsprings and they are dependent upon others for their existence. Climatic and geographical changes forces living organism to fight with the members of its own species to get enough water and nutrition. Reproduction is very important for all living beings. A tree which produces only a few seeds has to struggle with a plant that produce myriad seeds. There are plants that propagate their seeds with the help of birds. The plants which produce more fleshy fruits attract birds and their chance for survival is higher.

All living organisms produce large number of offsprings. For food and other facilities they have to struggle with others. The prodigality shown in reproduction is a precaution because only a few of the young ones reach adulthood. Others are perished. If all the young plants and animals survived what will happen? There the struggle for existence become inevitable. The struggle will be between either the members of the same species or the members of different species. Some times living organisms fight with environment also.

Nature has a tendency to check the increase in number of any species. If this check is necessary for the existence of other species in that environment. The uncontrolled increase in the number of any species, eventually becomes precarious to the species itself. In anyway a natural control is inevitable.

Carl Linnaeus the famous naturalist who started the classification of living things in a scientific method had made very interesting calculation. Linnaeus imagined a plant with a life period of one year produced only two seeds. (This is only a hypothetical condition since no plant produce only two seeds) Next year their seedlings produced two and so on and in twenty years there should be a million plants. Darwin quotes this calculation in his book. Again he goes on describing the breeding pattern of elephants, which is one the slowest breeder in the animal world. Imagine that an elephant starts breeding at age of thirty and goes on breeding till ninety years old. A pair of elephants bring forth six offsprings during that period, all surviving till hundred years old, so after a period of 740-750 years there would be nearly 19 million elephants alive descended from the first pair!

After stating such hypothetical situations Darwin comes to realistic world. After the discovery of America, some Europeans visited that land and took some plants from there to India since they got favourable conditions there these plants had spread, as Dr. Falconer informed Darwin, from Kanyakumari to Himalayas. The conditions have been highly favourable, there had been lesser destruction of the old and young and nearly all young had been able to reproduce This explains the rapid increase of these plants.

If this happens to all living organisms what will be the result? The surface earth will be filled with them no doubt. So at least some part of the young ones should be perished to enable the others to live better. Domestic animals are well protected. So their death rate is lesser. At the same time we slaughter them for nutrition purpose. In that way their population is checked.

Sometimes in nature mass destruction of living things occurs. In that situation the chances of survival is more or less equal to organisms with high breeding rate and lower breeding rate. Suppose a plant produce one seed which get favourable conditions for growth. Then it will grow and products next generation. Suppose another plant producing large number of seeds. If the conditions are unfavourable not a single seed would grow into a new plant.

Unfavourable climatic conditions and shortage of food tend living organism to engage in competition. In this competition all organisms try to win. Their struggle may be among the members of one species or among members of two species belonging to one genus. Sometimes competition takes place between species belonging to two geneva. For example, there is a possibility of competition between Herbivorous animals living in one habitat. In a habitat some animals feed on other animals. In a prey predator relationship we know that the number of species of the prey should be larger than the number of predator. Otherwise both the prey and predator would be terminated. So in this competition none is to lose and none is to win. It should continue eternally.

If there is a winner in the struggle existence who will be that? Of course the organisms with favourable adaptations will come out as winners. All organisms develop and exhibit small and continuous variations. These variations help them to adapt successfully with its environments.

Suppose a drastic change comes to the climate of a particular area. This change affects all living organisms seen there some of them will decrease in number and some will become extinct. Since all plants and animals are interdependent the decrease in the number of one species affects other species also. If this area is not an isolated one. The species from neighbouring area will migrate there. This migration also make changes in the existing organic relations. If the area is isolated from neighbouring places, that is separated by mountains or waters the organism already living there start living adjusting themselves with the changed habitat. Here the variation that help to adjust with the changed habitat is protected and inherited by the offsprings. Charles Darwin named this process "Natural selection" in the sense that favourable adaptation are always selected by nature. Unfavourable adaptations are not inherited and gradually disappears from earth.

Geological changes leads to variations. Natural selection is based on these variations. Man carefully select favourable variations appear in domestic animals and gradually transform them into new varieties. If man can do this within a short span by adding up individual difference the Nature which has incomparably larger time for action can do it for more easily. Darwin has no doubt about it.

Man who works with selection in domestic animals acts on external or visible characters. According to Darwin nature cares nothing of appearances except in so far they are useful to the organism. Darwin says that nature is careful about every internal organ. Morphological structure and the whole machinery of life. Man selects only for his own benefits. Nature selects only for the well being of the plant or animal. Nature is very particular that the selected adaptations should be most suitable for the organism to live in particular habitat. So only most favourable variations are selected by nature. As a result the structure and characters of the plant or animal changes. These changes are so slow and gradual, in the first stage they remain unnoticed. These changes are inherited by the next generation. Through generations the descendents become totally different from their ancestors. Darwin declared without hesitation that the plants and animals that lived in olden times were quite different from those we see now.

As stated earlier in the struggle for existence there is no winner or loser. The species which have better modification are selected by nature. The only parameter of the selection is its adaptations. The organisms selected by nature genetically transfer their modifications or adaptations to the next generation. Herbert Spencer the renowned Philosopher named this process as "Survival of the fittest" From the third edition onward Darwin used this phrase also along with, struggle for existence" in his *the origin of species*.

All the structural peculiarities and characteristic feature that we now observe in plants and animals are the accumulated variations selected by nature. Darwin put forward several examples to substantiate this point. The insects and cater pillars that feed on green leaves usually have green colour. The insects live on twigs and dead leaves are brown in colour. Here colour is an adaptation that help them to escape from predators. This colourisation is a result of natural selection. The colour of these organisms help them to adapt themselves to their habitat. This modification is preserved by nature and their offsprings inherited it. The colour and scent of some fruits give them better chance for propagation. The thorny covering of certain fruits give them protection from being eaten by animals.

Natural selection can work on animals at any stage of life. The eggs, larvas and pupa of a butterfly are found in circumstances most suitable for their life. Distribution of pollengrains through wind or by insects is encouraged by nature because they enable cross pollination. Nature never allows unfavourable modifications to be retained by natural selection.

Here Darwin presents two hypothetical examples. The first example is a variety of a wolf which is very strong and quick. This variety lives in an area where deers are plenty. The wolves those can run faster than others only could catch the deers. The agile and quick wolves are selected by nature. Their next generation will be more agile and quicker. The others who could not run faster would not get enough food. Gradually they would be terminated. Man has created strong and agile hounds through the process of artificial selection. So as Darwin observes nature can do this in a better way through centuries.

Then see another example. Insects are so fond of nectar formed between the petals of flowers. They come and sit on the flowers to suck it. At that time pollen grains get stuck on its body. Carrying this pollen grains the insect visit another flower. This enables cross pollination. Seeds formed through cross pollination are healthier and more productive than the seeds produced through self pollination. So nature promotes cross-pollination. Flowers with bright colour and strong smell attract insects. So the plants produce such flowers have better chance for survival. In the same way, the insects whose mouth parts are better adapted to suck the nector are protected by natural selection. Insects which have no such adaptation gradually perish.

The favourable modifications that help the organism to live in accordance with its environment is selected by the nature. But we can see that, at least in some cases some modifications turn to be precarious to the individual. Haven't you seen peacocks walthing labouriously holding the long blue green tail feathers. The cock's alarm could be a signal to its enemies like fox and jackal. Ths stag's large horn might be a barrior for its running? Still nature protect them as a favourable adaptions. Is nature mistaken here? Darwin says no.

Individual species fight with each other not only for food and dwelling space but also for mates. Usually male individuals engage in the fight for females. The winner will take her. They produce offsprings. The loser either die or become invalid. In any case the loser won't reproduce. Darwin called this process as 'Sexual selection' Though sexual selection is not as strong as Natural selection. Only a bold and strong male produce offsprings. That is sexual selection always allows the victor to breed. A hornless stag or spurless cock have a poor chance of leaving numerous offsprings. Male carnivores animals usually fight for females and we can see that they are well armed. But even some kind of beetles fights for a certain female. In most case the female sits and watches the struggle as an unconcerned bebolder. In the end she goes with the victor. Some animals develop some kind of defence mechanism through means of sexual selection. The mane of the lion acts as a shield. In a war as Darwin says shields are as important as sword or spear.

Sexual selection in birds takes place rather peacefully. In most cases the male bird attracts the female through sweet music. Some birds exhibit colourful feathers before the female. Peacock is the best example. Man in a short time make selection to give beauty and elegant plumes to his small chikcs according to his standard of beauty. Darwin had no doubt that female by selecting, during thousands of generations the most melodious or beautiful males according to their standard of beauty. Here natural selection works through the female birds. Darwin believed that male and female of any animal have the same general habit of life but difference in structure, colour or ornament, such difference have been mainly caused by sexual selection.

Again Darwin describes the circumstances under which the natural selection takes place. Let's listen to him.

7
The Tree of Life

Natural selection comes into effect only when there are differences between the individuals. When the number of individuals in a certain species increases tremendouly there develops variations in them on which natural selection can work. Nature allows long periods of time for the work of natural selection but it does not grant an indefenite period. Darwin says that all organic beings are striving to sieze on its place in the economy of nature. If one species does not become modified and improved in a corresponding degree with its competitors it will be perished

Men select plants and animals for their use. They select beneficial species and destroy species which are not useful to them. Nature has no such goals. But nature also does it in the same way. Nature destroys speices those have no favourable modification. As a result favourable variations are inherited by offsprings. As a result after a few generations only improved varieties remain.

A vast area can be divided into smaller areas. Each smaller area will have different features. The inhabitanuts living these smaller area develop adaptations favourable in that area. These adaptations are promoted by natural selection. So each region gets variations different from their ancestors. But if these different variants interbreed their adaptations will be mixed and the result will be species with average quality. So nature wants to prevent the chances of interbreeding. This is done by different variants living in different regions, different species mating during different seasons and by each species accepting males only from the same species. In isolated area the number of individuals in each speices will be lesser. Variations also will be lesser here. So chances of new species originating in isolated areas are rare. That is why we find lesser number of species in islands and other isolated places.

In an organic world of wide and open area the number of individuals in all species will be greater than that of an isolated area. The chances of new species with better modifications originating area also greater there. when the number of species increase the environment became more complicated and severe struggle for existence takes place there. Under these cirumstnaces new species with modified features will appear. These modifications help them to adapt themselves with environment in a better way. After a few generations the species remaining in that area will be entirely different from their ancestors.

The lesser the number of species the lesser the struggle for existence will be. That is the case of small islands and fresh water ponds. The species living there are not much affected by natural selection. They need not be modified much because the chances of extinction is less. So some ancient species are found in fresh water lakes. They haven't under gone much modification. Darwin called these species which show archaic features as "living fossils" Darwin mentions two varieties of fresh water fish in his book named as ornithorhynchus and Lepidosiren. They remained in a confined area and were exposed to less variation and less competition.

In the later years naturalist have discovered some more 'living fossils.' Do you know what is a fossil? Fossils are remainings of animals and plants that lived in prehistoric period. The word fossils originated from the Latin word Fosilium which means something escavated. This living fossils are found in area natural selection was less active. From this you get the answer to the question why rare varieties of animals and plants are found in Australia and Newzealand.

In ancient world Australia and Newzealand were part of a larger continent, now we call Asia. Kangaroos hoped everywhere in that vast land. Centuries passed and great geological changes occured. Australia and Newzealand drifted away from Asia. Kangaroos living in Asia had to compete with many other animals around them. They had to face severe climatic changes also. As a result they underwent many variations. The variations most suitable their survival were protected by natural selection. Gradually the descendents of Kangaroos evolved into a quite different animal. In a small island like Australia because of lack of competition the Kangaroos did n't undergo drastic changes. So we still see them carrying their young ones in their marsupiuns (bag of skin) as in the ancient world Kangaroos and platipus, the egg laying mammal are the relics of natural selection that ended midway.

In the living world severe fight occurs between closely related species. When a new species or variety arise its close relative becomes a strong competitor. Man, when he gets an improved variety of plant or animal he discards all the ancestral species. Our indigenous varieties of paddy were disappeared following the introduction of Hybrid varieties. In fact when farmers get Hybrid variety of seeds they fail to protect indigenous varieties. As a result the indegenous varieties are on the verge of extinct. Darwin justifies the extinction of plants and animals from earth because according to him the removal of old varieties is highly necessery. Then only new and improved varieties will take their place. Once a variety of black cows flourished in the yorkshire county of Britain. This variety became extinct and in its place came a new variety of cows with long horns. Darwin calls this as an incident of historical importance. The latter also did not last for long. There arrived another variety with short horns. The cows with long horns disappeared as if they were terminated by an epidemic, Says Darwin quoting an agriculture scientist. If man can terminate a number of species within a short span of time can't nature annihilate uncountable species in the period of millions of years.

We have seen that any number of variation can occur in a species. The variants, differ in morphological structure and living habits move away from their original habitat and find new surroundings to live in. Their efficiency to exploit the new habitat depends upon the variations they gained. If their adaptation help them to exploit the new habitat in a better way they flourish in that particular area.

See the example of a carnivorous animal. In favourable conditions they breed and produce large number of individuals. Under a certain environment their number reaches a maximum limit. It the species wants to expand further it has to change its way of life and feeling habits. The descendent of an ancient animal that lived in caves and hunted stags can be an animal living in trees and feeding on insects. The descendents move away from the habitat where their ancestors flourished. This kind of diversification shows a basic nature of Nature.

A group of ancestral organisms passing through thousands of years produce a number of variations. Again modification come to them and all these changes leads to formation of new species. In *origin of species* Darwin gives the exmaple of a large tree which represent the relations of living organisms. The green and budding twigs represent existing species. The dead branches represent extinct species. At each period of growth the growing twigs try to branch out on all sides and overlop surrounding twigs. In the same manner species and groups of species have at all times overmastered others species in great struggle for existence. When the tree was young, the branches now seen were only buds and budding twigs. The connection of former buds and present buds by ramifying branches represent the connection of all extinct and living species. When the tree was bush the twigs flourished on it. Of them only two or three have grown into branches. They bear other branches. Some branches have fallen down and decayed. They represent whole groups of organisms which have no living representative now. Two or three healthy living branches show that of the species which lived during long past periods and have left living and modified descendents. There are some thin branches arising from a fork low down in the tree, which because of some favourable condition saved fatal competition and still alive represent living fossils. They have survived the struggle for existence by living in isolated areas.

As buds gives rise to fresh buds and if healthy branches overtop on all sides over feebler branches. Darwin says that the great "Tree of Life" is also like this which fills the earth's crust with dead and broken branches and covers the surface ever branching and beautiful ramifications. It stands there eternally.

This is not a poet's imagination but the discovery of a Scientist with extraordinary power of observation. At the same time it contains a revolutionary's vision also. Darwin came forward with his ideas at a time when the theory of creation was at its height. Even scientist believed that the creator created everything independently Darwin asserted that if we trace back we will reach a common ancestor. Can white people who believed that God created them to rule over others tolerate the idea that the white and the Negroes of Africa originated from a common ancestor lived in the distant past? At that time it was a real revolutionary idea. In fact in the first edition of his book Darwin mentions the word God nowhere. In the second edition he uses the word creator only once. It is believed that Darwin tactfully did this in order to pacify his critics. So most people like to accept the first edition as the real Darwinism.

We have already seen that Darwin was not the first naturalist to advocate the theory of evolution. His predecessors include Buffton, Lammarck and his grandfather Erasmus Darwin. But the idea that due to variation a species transforms into another and Nature directs this transformation was an original idea. Its credit goes to Charles Darwin. Natural selection is Darwin's own idea. Alfred wallace knew nothing of Darwin's ideas when he independently reached the theory of Natural selection. But in the later years Wallace never claimed it as his brainchild. It is quite interesting to note that when wallace worte a book on Natrual Selection he named it "Darwinism.

Alfred Wallace was a brillant naturalist. But in his later years he gave up natural science and started reserach on ghosts and spirits. He regularly visited people who claimed the ability to communicate with ghosts. He even wrote book on it. In this book he says that he had witnessed a man taking the photo of a spirit. No doubt Wallace lacked the scientific attidude and way of thinking that Darwin always had.

Natural Selection was Darwin's favourite idea. But he never claimed that it is only means of evolution. He said natural selection was one of the main causes of evolution. There might be other causes also and that is the way of scientist

Darwin knew well that the victorian society would not accept his ideas offhanded by. To silence the criticisms he had to put forward undeniable evidences. He collected these amazing evidences through a period of two decades. when we go through these evidences we will bow our head before the dedication and determination of this great scientist.

$$8$$

Horse, Ass and Zeebra

Darwin's visit to Galapagos islands was the most important turning points of his voyage. He got the germ of his idea of evolution there. He himself had stated it. The earth and all the living beings undergo continuous evolution Darwin had no doubt about it. But he had to convince others also. With this purpose in mind, Darwin sent all his collections to England. He wanted his specimens reach England before him. He was ready to explain all his collections.

The changes in the enviornment leads to variations. And these variations are inherited by the offsprings. This is the main cause of evolution and biodiversity. Nature selects individuals with favourable adaptations. We have already seen that, Darwin calling it Natural selection. The finches on Galapagos islands gave him the first clue of evolution. We can try to explain the diversity in Finches of Galapagos islands in the light of Natural Selection.

The ancsestors of the Finches might have arrived in the islands long long ago. There were similarites between them and the Finches of main land. At the sametime the Finches on the Islands were different in their own way. The Finches on the different islands were themselves different from are another- what conclusion could one reach from this? The different groups of birds must have had common ancestry but because of various reasons they evolved into diverse groups. As these groups had no contact with the others they independently changed and developed variations. Finally they had become different species. Finches in each island evolved according to the living conditions there. They developed adaptations to cope with the environment of that island. These adaptations were inherited by next generation or Nature selected birds with favourable adaptations.

As far as the birds are concerned beak is the most important organ. Suppose in a certain island there existed some trees which bore fruits with very hard outer covering. Only those brids which have very strong beak would be able to break the hard external covering of the fruit and eat it. These birds could live and reproduce. Their offsprings would have bigger and stronger beaks. The offsprings without big strong beaks wouldn't live long to breed and produce younger ones. The next generation of birds would have even stronger and larger beaks than those of the birds which have initially survived. Gradually these Finches would be evolved as a new species quite different from birds of the neighbouring islands. In each island the enviornment is different and because of the difference in their habitat the Finches on each island had evolved away from those on the other islands.

How did the favourable adaptations develop in an individual? Darwin laid out his conclusion in a way they appeared to be open ended. You can add any more conclusions to them. He made use of the observations of several contemporary naturalists.

Continuous use or disuse make variations in the living beings. The organs under continuous use enlarges considerably. The organs which are not in use diminishes and disappears. Here Darwin seems to agree with Lamarck. Lamarck might have influenced Darwin. Darwin considered him a great man who first proposed the idea that the changes in the organic world are governed by certain natural laws.

Darwin considered disuse, not use the major factor that influence Natural Selection. The one problem that we face here is that we don't know which organs were in great use and which were not in use in ancestral animals. But Darwin believed that we can solve the mystery of vestiges seen in the body of some living beings using this theory. One of the greatest anomally in the living world is the birds that can not fly. Wild geese and ostriches belong to this group. Most of these birds are inhabitants of islands. Since there were no enemies to attack them they need not have to fly long distance. Continuous disuse resulted in diminished feathers and their wings became feeble and useless as for as flying was concerned. The ostriches lived on the main land. But we know that its body is too big to fly. They could run very fast and fight the enemies using its strong legs. Natural Selection protected ostriches with weak wings and strong legs. Gradually their ancestors who might have flown were eradicated completely from earth.

Most of the burrowing animals have very poor eyesight. This condition is the combined effect of disuse and natural selection. Darwin found some burrowing animals having their eyes covered with a membrane. This membrane is meant to proect their eyes from loose earth falling into the eyes. This membrane is a desirable adaptation that help the animal to adjust with the habitat. Their eyes become diminished due to disuse and Natural Selection might have encouraged it.

The animals permanently live in darkness usually have no eyes. They might have lost their eyes because of disuse. "Darwin, with the help of other naturalists understood that almost everywhere the cave dwelling animals are usally blind. If god had created these animals specially to live in dark caves, the cave dwellers should be alike in every sense in all parts of the world. But that is not the case. In each area the cave dwellers are very similar to the animals living outside the cave in that particular habitat. What does it mean? The ancestors of these animals lived there outside the caves. Some of its variation for reasons unknown went into the caves and started to live there. Because of continuous disuse they lost their eyesight. This character is inherited by their offspring. Thus there happened to be generations without eyesight. Darwin believed that only Natural Selection could explain these phenomena.

Each species is adapted to the climate of its environment. Species from arctic or temperate region can't endure the climate of tropical region. But almost all the domestic animals are origInated in one region and transported to other parts of world with the help of man. Wherever they reach they adapt themselves with the climate of that region and reproduce. So we can assume that living beings can tolerate the climatic variations to a large extent rate. Rats are seen from temperate zone to tropical zone. Darwin says that the seeds of pinetrees collected from the different heights of the Himalayas sprouted and grew well in England. He again claims that there is enough evidences to substantiate that the ancestors of Elephants and Rhinos lived in glacial climates where as the living speices are seen in tropical and subtropical regions. The ability to endure the most different climates is an innate nature of almost all living organisms. When they are forced to live in particular environment they develop adaptations to cope with the climate in that environment.

What effects the organisms adaptation to climate? Is it their habit or Natural Selection? Species living in a particular area will develop adaptations for the climate there. At the same time the offspring born with favourable adaptations only will survive in that particular area. So we can not rule out Natural Selection completely. The variations, let it be by use or disuse or by life style of the species, natural selection plays a decisive role in it.

The body of an organism is a structure formed by the association of different organs. When a variation occurs to one organ and it is encouraged by Natural Selection it affects other organs also. That is when one part gets modified the other parts are also modified. The variations of structure arising in the young ones or larvae naturally tend to affect the Nature animal. Darwin believed that the defects occured in the early embryonic stage affects the whole being. Darwin observed that some physical defects appear in a correlated fashion in some species. In cats complete whiteness and blue eyes always go with deafness. Darwin always found Natural Selection as a process helpful to the species. So Darwin confesses that he could not understand how these correated variations help a species. If he had known the laws of heridity he would not have made such a statement. We can come to that later.

When natural selection causes enlargement of one part of the body some other parts get reduced. As some naturalists say there is a simple economics behind it. In order to spend on one side Nature is forced to economics on otherside. When one variety of cabbage yeild plenty of foliage, another varieity give abundant supply of oil bearing seeds. These two qualities are seldom seen in same plants. Darwin explains it that nourishment flows to one part in excess, it rarely flows at least in excess to other parts. When fruits itself gains largely in size and quality they bear lesser number of seeds. The cows yielding much milk do not produce large amount of meat. Darwin shows his integrity by saying this reduction may caused by disuse, not Natural Selection. He shows the example of parasites living in other organisms. They have developed mouth parts in order to receive food, but other parts become reduced due to disuse. According to Darwin Natural Selection tends in long run to reduce any part of a living being as soon as it becomes through changed habits superflows, without enlarging a corresponding part. The other way round also happens in nature. Natural Selection succeeds in enlarging one part of the body without reducing another part.

All individuals belonging to one species share some common features. A genus include more than one species. So the members of two or more species belonging to one genus also will have some common traits. According to Darwin the characterisitc features of a genus is much older than that of the spceies. The species in a genus share the features received from their common ancestor which are no more variable. The variations between the species of a genus are comparatively new. They will again undergo changes. As Darwin states specific characters are more variable than generic characters.

Sometimes different species belonging to one genus exhibit similar variations. We can easily explain this by accepting the idea of common ancestor. Again we can see some variation of a certain species showing the characters of another related species. This all happens because they have descended from a common ancestor. Darwin claims he has collected a number of evidences in this regard and discloser his idea of writing another book on this after completing *The origin of species*. Unfortunately that didn't happen.

Darwin gives only one example here. He himself calls it very interesting and complicated. The ass sometimes has distinct transverse stripes on its legs and shoulder like those on the legs and shoulder of zeebra. Some types of stripes are sometimes seen on horses also. Dawin made studies about the horses not only in Engliand but in India also. Coloured poole, a military officer from India reported Darwin that the kattywar breed of horses found in north-west part of India are generally stripped. A horse without such stripe is not considered ad purely-bred. In mules, produced by cross breeding horse and ass also appear these stripes.

What can be deduced from this? The stripes that appear in horse ass, mule and the like species must be a trait inherited from their common ancestor. The morphological feature of a common ancestor who lived long past appear in its descendents. Thousands and thousands of years ago there lived an striped like Zeebra but quite different from modern Zeebra is the common parent of our domestic horse, ass and Zeebra; Darwin states confidently. If all these animals are created sperately how can these stripes appear on them in the same way? How do long lost traits of anceient ancestors appear in younger generation. The theory that all modern living organisms share some common ancestors can answer these questions satisfactorily. Darwin goes on with his evidences.

9
The Unknown Ancestor

Darwin was well aware of the questions that might have risen against his theory. He himself had asked those questions several times. If all the species that we see now has been formed from old species by modification and development, where are the transitional varieties

This is a very important question. Natural Selection preserves species with favourable modification. When a new form with better modification arises its less improved parent form and other less improved varieties has to come into competion with the improved spceies. In the struggle for existence parents and all transitional varieties get extermentated. If there existed some transitional varieties the number will be lesser and their habitat will be limited. So any change that affects the enviornment or climate will affect them harmfully. Since the aim of Natural Selection is to promote will adapted species, this transitional varieties become extinct.

These extinct species should have left their remainings on or under the surface of earth. During Darwin's time paleontology and research on fossils were in a state of infancy. The principles of Geology, put forward by Charles Lyell was not popularly accepted Darwin states only the future historian will recognise that Lyell had created a revolution in Natural Science. Darwin knew that fossils play a critical role in proving his theory of organic evolution. But the fossils deposited on earth's crust had been destroyed and disintegrated by the action of several agencies. They are sometimes dissolved in rain water or carried down the slopes during heavy rain, in some place by wind. Then they are transported by streams or rivers. So it is very difficult the find the fossil remaining in the places where the ancestral species and transitional varieties lived.

When we see two species very similar to each other we begin to imagine a transtional variety linking the two. That is not the correct way, says Darwin. Both species were descended from an unknown ancestor lived long ago. We want to find out the transitional variety that led from the ancestor to the living species through variations. The living species now we see are not originated from another existing species. But both these species were originated from a common ancestor. So we have to find out the link between the ancestor and the exisiting species. offsprings undergo continuous variation and gradually become new species. This is a slow process and take a long time. By this time the ancestors might have become extict. A species one's extinct never comes back.

If living organisms are not available we have to go in search of fossils Mother earth has kept them in between her various stratas. But Darwin was convinced that these fossil collection was not sufficient to make an elaborate study on the history of living organisms. During that period only a small portion of the surface of the earth was geologically explored.

Collected fossils were in most cases broken and disintegrated and most of them were collected from one spot organisms with soft bodies left no fossils. The bodies reach the bottom of the sea decay and disappear there if no sedimentation occured. When the earth's plates move the preserved fossils are destroyed. Fossils are never found in uniform distribution in the different stratas of earth.

Sometimes a stratum without fossil is found sandwitched between two fossil-rich stratas. Even the stratum seen rich in fossils in one place would be found without any fossil in another region. So it is very difficult to get a complete picture from these fossil records. Again, the fermentation of new species is a very slow process. If all the transitional forms were to be embedded in one stratum, it should be very thick and that particular species might have lived in the same region for a long period. When a species migrated to another region the fossil records would be incomplete. Even though it returned after an interval the changes occured during the interim period would not be recorded there. Darwin even accuses. Nature of having a hidden agenda to prevent man from finding out the intermediate varieties.

By the first half of nineteenth century paleontologists had discovered fossils as old as 360 million years. But Darwin and his friends believed that life existed even before that. But the ancient organisms were of soft bodies so that their fossils were not embedded on rocks or muddy layer of earth. Charles Lyell, the famous Geologist once said that he looked at Geological record as a history of the world imperfectly kept and written in changing dialects; of this history we possess the last volume alone, relating only to two or three countries. Of this volume only here and there a short chapter had been preserved, and of each page only here and there a few lines. Even in this twenty first century we haven't got the full volumes of that record. Then how can one find fault with Charles Darwin for not giving a complete picture's of organic evolution?

Though Darwin quotes Lyell's metaphor in the chapter on Geological records, he presents his case in a most perfect way. The fossils found in the oldest layers were of simplest structure. Later species become more developed than the older ones. They are better adapted to cope with the changed climate. If a species existed 200 million years ago, is brought to live with modern species, in the struggle for existence the ancient species will be exterminated.

Some species of animals were brought to Britain from Newzealand. They did not flourish in Britain. At the same time the species taken to Newzealand from Britain reproduced and flourished there in a very good manner. This was because the species in Britian were more developed than the species of Newzealand. In other words the Newzealand species were rather primitive. So they could not adapt themselves with the new environment. A few fossils were discovered from some cover of Australia. These fossils show similarity to the animals of the class to which Kangaroos belong. This shows that the present day species were gradually evolved from some ancestral species and Darwin claims that fossils provide strong evidence in this case.

Darwin presents another evidence from Embryology. For this Darwin depended on the studies made by Louris Agazzi, who was a renowned Naturalist and Paleontologist. But it is interesting to note that Agassiz was always an an Darwinist. Being a close friend of Geroge Curier he also was an advocate of theory of creation. He strongly believed that all species including man was created by God independently. He never agreed with Darwin's idea of common ancestor. But Darwin had little hesistation to make use of Agassiz's discoveries to justify his theory. Agassiz made a vast study about fossils. He discovered the embryos of modern species took very much like the fossils of their related ancestors. To Darwin who was in search of intermediate varieties this was a great news.

An embryo often shows resemblance to the structure of his less modified ancestor. Now we can guess that the adult stage of the extinct variety resembled the embryo of the existing varieties of the same class. Modern species reveal the different stages passed during evolution through the different embryonic stages. According to Darwin this is an undeniable evidence for the existence of a common ancestor. In the embryonic stage the homologous organs are more or less look alike. They become widely different only in matured state.

Darwin wanted the fossils of prehistoric organisms to prove this point without doubt, which were not available at that time. Now we know that after Darwin's time both Embryology and Paleontology progressed very much and they provide strong evidences for organic evolution.

The embryos of closely related species show strong resemblance between them. Mammals, birds and reptiles come under the division of vertebrates. Their embryos in the early stages are so similar, that as Agassiz states it is difficult to recognise one from the other. He believed that it was a law of Nature. But Darwin took it as a strong evidence of evolution. There is resemblance between the larvae of beetle, butterfly and housefly. In adult stage we know that they are quite different from one another. The embryos by gradual modification become the adult organism. That is the same way the ancient species by gradual modification, and by Natrual Selection become modern speices. The modifications appear in adults not in the embryonic stage. So embryos of species belonging to the same class show resemblance to one another. The embryos exhibit the general characters of their common ancestor. That is why the embryos of cow, horse, bat and whale look alike.

The similarity in the morphology of related species also provide a good evidence for organic evolution. Observe the hands of men forelimbs of mouse and horse and the fins of whales and wings of bats. Each of them are different from others in their own way. Though their external appearance are different they have a general pattern internally. The size and shape of the bones are different. But they are joined in the same way. How all this happened?

Darwin says that he can explain this in the light of Natural Selection. The forlimb of mouse and the wing of the bat and fin of the whale are the modified form of an organ of a common ancestor. When the environment changed their external appeerence changed to adapt with the new habitat. But their internal structure remained same. The difference occured because of the transformation through Natural Selection. Darwin believed that both embrology and morphology can explain organic evolution and biodiversity in a scientifically intelligible way.

Darwin's great work *The origin of species* was the result of twenty two years hard work and systematic observation. Charles Darwin presented his theory with clarity and confidience and he had answer to every objection that anti Darwinist might arise. Why no mammals are seen in isolated islands except those could fly like bats? Why didn't God create frogs in the ponds and lakes on the islands? Darwin asked similar questions to his opponents. But none of their answers are registered in history with significance.

Darwin assumed that all animals are descended from a common ancestor. He also believed that plants and animals share a common ancestry. In the long past they descended as two groups from a common ancestor. The cellular structure gives enough evidence in this case. In chemical structure, cell division and growth we can find striking similarities. All living organisms share the 'same soul.' This is an oriental vision. But the great Charles Darwin also agrees with it.

Towards the end of the book Darwin politely says that he has opened a grand and almost untrodden field of enquiry for his successors. He expected many naturalists would come along the path he had opened. In the future Darwin saw open fields for far more important researches. Darwin who made these prophecies did not know what was happening in a nearby European country. At a time when Darwin confessed his own ignorance of the laws of heridity, another man had already discovered them.

Gregor Johan Mendel is now known as the father of Genetics. Though contemporaries Darwin and Mendel never met. If they had met, what effect it would have been on life science?

10

A Priest's Experiments

Gregor Mendel was born in the state of Moravia in erstwhile Czekoslovakia. His father was a poor farmer. He joined the university and studied Mathematics and Natural science. Because of financial problems he could not complete his graduation. 1843 he joined as a priest in St. Thomas Monastry in the town of Brunn. This town is now in Austria. He began working as teacher in the school attached to the monastry.

Mendel conducted his famous experiments on Hybridisation in the vegetable garden of this monastry. He selected garden pea plants for his experiments as variations are very conspicuous in these plants. Different variety of pea plants were grown in the garden. Some of them with very long stem, and others, variety dwarf. Some plants had red flowers and some others white. Some plants produced seeds white in colour and some produced seeds with dots on them. The Kernel of one type was white in colour and some other yellow. Mendel selected plants having different traits and did cross pollination in them. He collected seeds from these selected plants and continued his experiment in the next generation. He got amazing results.

Before coming to the results we have to know a little more about his experiments. In one of his initial experiments Mendel selected plants with tall stem and crossed them with dwarf varitey. He collected and planted seperately. In the second generation there were only plants with alongated stem. The trait dwarfness had disappeared. Mendel went on with his experiments. This time he allowed the plants of the second generation to self pollinate when the seeds from these plants germinated there were tall plants and dwarf ones. The traits found in the first generation reappeared in the third generation! Of course these traits had come through second generations. But they were visible nowhere there. They lay dormant some where in the second generation.

Mendel repeated his experiments using plants different in other qualities. He got the same result. Mendel collected all the data, analysed the results and kept the records of his experiments to the minute detail. It was in 1856 that Mendel started his experiments. By 1863 based on his experiments Mendel formulated certain principles. He understood that the heriditory characters are transferred from parents to offsprings following a particular pattern. We should remember that Mendel proposed his principles of inheritance without any knowledge of either genes or chromosome. At the same time, like Darwin Mendel also knew that he was travelling along an untrodden path. So as stated earlier he kept full records of his experiments. Besides this he kept the seeds of each generation in seperate labelled packets. It is said that Mendel had kept more than thousand packets in his room. It was only after 1863 Mendel started speaking about his experiments. He was ready to send the seeds to other Botanists to do the experiments and verify the results.

Let's examine Mendel's pea plants once again. In the third generation elongated variety and dwarf variety appeared in a fixed ratio. In the third generation one by fourth of the total plants were dwarf. Others were plants with elongated stems. When self pollination was allowed, the dwarf plants of third ganeration produced only dwarf ones. Others produced both varieties. Mendel repeated his experiments taking into consideration other traits like colour of the flower, colour of the seeds, shape of the kernels etc. In all cases in result was the same. Based on these experiments Gregor Mendel formulated his principles which later became the basis of genetics.

Mendel assumed that in all organisms each trait is controlled by a pair of factors. He knew nothing about genes. So he called them factors of the pair of factors one is dominant and the other is necessive. Only one factor is active at one time and the other remains dormant. When the factors deciding height and dwarfism come together, the dominant factor is that of height. So plant appears with elongated stem. The factor deciding dwarfism remains dormant inside the plant. When reproductive cells or gametes are formed these pair of factors seggregates and the gametes gets only one factor.

Before coming to his cross breeding or Hybridisation Mendel had done enough home work. First he made sure that both the paternal and maternal plants were pure. That is they carry only one type of factor for each trait. For this he allowed self pollination in those plants and verified that the plants with elongated stem produced only same type of plants and from dwarf variety only dwarfs were produced. So Mendel's first generation had the factors determining either height or dwarfness.

Mendel's cross breeding can be graphically represented in this way. Here the letters 'T' shows the factor for height and 't' stands for dwarfness. You know that in plants the pollen grains bear male gametes and ova bear female gametes. All gametes of the taller plants carry the factor 'T' and dwarf plants carry factor 't'. When they were crossed the result will be as given below.

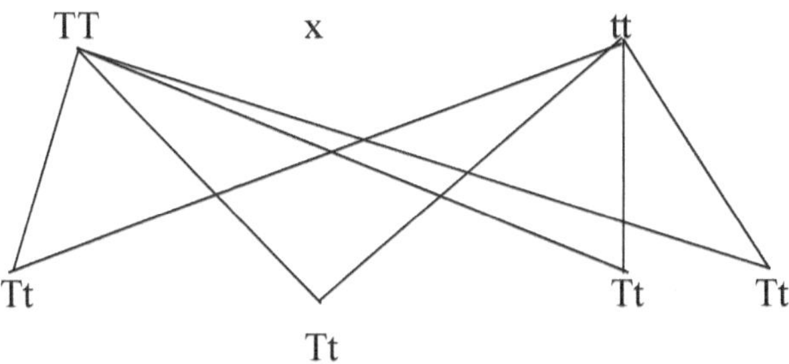

Here all plants bear the factor 'T' and 't'. But 'T' is the dominant factor and in its presence, the recessive factor 't' becomes dormant. So all plants will be tall. When these tall plants were allowed to pollinate themselves there would be two types of gametes. Half of the bearing 'T' factor and other half bearing 't' factor. Their fusion would be like this.

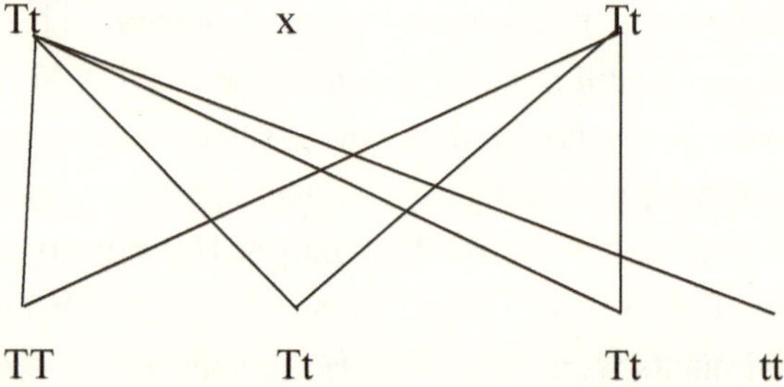

of these four plants three would be tall and the fourth one dwarf.

Mendel analysed his results and in his own way found out the laws of inheritance. Mendel presented this laws in a talk he made at the Natural science Society of Brunn. Then it was published in Austrian Journal of Natural History society of Brunn in 1866. Seven years had passed since the first edition of *The origin of species* was published. By this time Darwin had become very famous. After the publication of *The origin of species* the European scientific world was after Darwin. But nobody paid attention to Mendel's law of inheritance. Darwin who belonged to an aristocratic family had got strong and influential supporters. Being a poor priest Mendel found no godfather.

Mendel wrote continueosly to all well known contemporary naturalists about his discovery. He even sent the copy of his paper to some of them. A few doubts were raised about his results by some scientists; but nobody encouraged him. Charles Darwin being the most illustrated contemporary of Mendel naturally received a copy of his paper. Unfortunately Darwin did not go through Mendel's paper. The interesting fact is that at that time Darwin was troubled with question, how genetic characters are passed from parents to offsprings. If he had read Mendel's paper he would have got the answer. It is quite an irony that Darwin who had the habit of reading the articles of unknown persons to Chinese Encyclopedia to get ideas supportive to his research left Mendel's paper unread.

1868 Darwin put forward a theory of heridity in one of his books. He called this theory 'Pangenisis' which has only historical value. According to this theory the cells in a living body produce minute particles called 'gemmules.' The modifications occured to an organ affects the gemmules in that organ. At the time of reproduction these gemmules are passed to the offsprings. In this way variations are transferred to one generation to another. Eventhough the idea came from Charles Darwin, the theory of Pangenisis didn't get much supporters. If Darwin had gone through the papers of Mendel he wouldn't have come out with this theory.

Let's go back to Gregor Mendel. The then scientific world was not developed enough to accept his principles of inheritance most scientists denied the importance of Mendelism because they were preoccupied with the gradual variation and Darwin's Natural Selection. Besides this, Mendel presented his ideas along with a lot of arithmetics. Naturalists found it baffling. They could not make out his exact idea and one of them advised a Mendel not mix Natural science with Mathematics.

In 1868 Mendel was appointed as the Abbot of the Monastry. He was forced to give up his teaching profession because as the head of the Monastry he had several responsibilities. He gave up his scientific research also. This might be because of lack of time or the lukeworm reception he got from the scientific world might have discouraged him. Another story is that Mendel started the second phase of his hybridisation experiments in rabbits. When Gregor Mendel, a Catholic priest started supervising the mating of rabbits and counting the litter objections arouse from several corners. They never understood that the priest had applied the same technique in pea-plants. Eventually Mendel was forced to wind up his experiments.

Mendel passed away in 1884. He received a grand funeral that suits an abbot. In the obituaries no one spoke about Mendel, the scientist. But Mendel's laws of Heridity was not destined to be buried with him. Mendelin got a rebirth in the first decade of twentieth century. It was at the cost of the greatest despair in the life of another great scientist.

11

Genes meet Darwin

Before the rediscovery of Mendelism we must know about another great discovery. It was made by a German Doctor by name August Wiesman. With this discovery Wiesman wiped off Lamarckism completely. Now it has only a historical importance.

August Wiesman was born on 17 January 1834 in Frankfurt, Germany. Though he was very much interested in scientific research his mother wanted him to be a doctor. So he joined the medical college. After graduating he went for military service. Then he returned to Frankfurt and served as private doctor of some aristccratic families.

All these time his mind was after scientific research. Evolution was one of his favourtie topics. He boldly declared that he was a Darwinist and wrote a book justifying Darwinism. But he did not agree with the idea that the modification caused by the changes in the enviornment pass genetically to the offsprings. He was doubtful about Natural Selection leading to the formation of new species. Wiesman thought the other way round. If there were no changes in the enviornment no variation would occur and there by no organic evolution. His rational mind revolted against it.

Wiesman conducted a series of interesting experiments. He cut the tails of a group of white rate that he had bred. When allowed to mate they produced young ones with tails. He repeated the experiment with second generation. Again young rats with tails were born. He repeated this experiment in five generations. Not a single rat was born without tail. He observed 901 baby rats. All of them had long tails. He was convinced that a change affecting the morphology of an animal will not be transferred genetically.

The reproductive cells or gametes are entirely different from the other cells of the body. It is these gametes that bear the hereditary characteristics to the next generation. A species exhibits the characters it received through the gametes. The characters acquired during the lifetime are never genetically transferred to the offsprings. This was Wiesman's theory. This theory made Lamarckian principles quite irrevelent. But Wiesman's theory became more intelligible only after the discovery of genes and DNA. Though Gregor Mendel is considered as the father of genetics the real germ of genetics lie in the theory proposed by Wiesman.

Wiesman put forward his theory in 1883. At the same time another scientist was conducting studies on the same subject. That was Prof. Hugo Devrier working in Amstardam University, Holland. Like Wiesman he also was interested in Darwinism. He modified Darwin's theory of Pangenesis and wrote a book on it namely *Intracellular pangenesis*. From 1892 onwards Devries was trying to develop new varieties of plants by Hybridisation. While doing this experiments he found out the way how heriditory characters pass from parents to offspring. That was the same laws formulated by Mendel. But Devries was quiet unaware of Mendel and his experiments.

Devries wanted to publish his discoveries. Before doing that he made a review of previous researches done in this field. By the way he came upon Mendel's paper. He was wonderstruck to find out that what he had discovered after long research lay spread out in those papers written by an unknown man, Gregor Mendel. Devries became desperate. Still he was unwilling to handover to ownership of his favourite ideas to Mendel. In 1900 he published his discoveries in a French journal.

Mendel's destiny did not follow Devries. His discovery attracted the attention of scientific world. But his property was questioned by another Botanist Karl Correns. Correns had already heard about Gregor Mendel and read his laws of inheritance. That happened in this way. Correns was a student of renowned Botanist Karl Nageli. Mendel used to write to Nageli explaining his experiments. Eventhough Nageli was an expert in the field of Hybridisation, he did not pay attention to Mendel's laws. Correns also had read Mendel's papers. He was not ready to allow another man snatching the credit of Mendel's discovery. Erich Von Shermac, another well known Dutch Botanist also supported Correns. Both of them argued that the credit of the discovery of Laws of Heredity should go to Gregor Mendel. Like Correns Shermac also had a Mendel 'connection.' His grandfather was Mendel's teacher at the University. Devries did not want himself to be dragged into a controversy. He agreed that he had rediscovered Mendalism.

In 1900, Thirty four years after his death scientific world recognised Mendel and his laws of Heredity. Now we honour him as the father of Genetics, because his discoveries became the basis of all progress and development in the field of Genetics. Now we learn that Huga Devries' Karl Correns and Erich Von Shermac rediscovered Mendelism.

In 1901 Devries made another major discovery. This time he need not have to share the credit with anybody. Variations are caused by a process called mutation taking place in reproductive cells. These variations are carried over to the next generation. That was Devries discovery. He called this phenomenon as 'mutation.' According to

Devries mutations are sudden changes, which are transferred to the next generation through reproductive cells. He could not makes out the real cause of mutation, but he assumed that it might be because of some sudden changes in its genetic materials.

The last decade of nineteenth century witnessed many important scientific discoveries. These discoveries steered science through the twentieth century and became the basis of almost all branches of science now we study. In 1895 Conrad Rontgen, a German physicist discovered a type of wonderful rays which could pierce into solid substances. It was named after Rontgen, but later known as x-rays Devries suggested that 'Rontgen rays' could cause mutation in living cells. After two or three decades it was proved beyond doubt that any kind of radiation could affect the genetic structure of species, and the variation caused by it whether adverse or beneficial would pass to the next generation.

In the early decades of twentieth century itself genes and chromosomes were discovered. The word 'gene' has a Darwin association. As stated earlier Devries modified Darwin's theory of Pangenisis, and coined a new term, 'Pangenes'. The word 'genes' now we know is derived from it.

Mendelism was rediscovered and Devries 'Theory of mutation' got wide acceptance. After that Genetics began to advance in leaps and bounds. To some extent Darwin's theory of 'Natural Selection" became a little insignificant. Some Naturalists argued that Evolution is not a slow process as Darwin said, but new species appear suddenly by mutation. Darwinists came forward to defend the theory of Natural selection. The two groups of Naturalists, that is mutation fans and Darwinists stuck on to their own ideologies stubburnly and did not want to recognise the other. It was Thomes Hunt Morgan, the famous American scientist made a consensus among them.

T H Morgan was a professor at Columbia University, America. He was doing some research in Geology. Once he met Devries at

Amstardam. The acquaintance with Devries persuaded Morgan to turn his attention towards Genetics. Both Devries and his theory of mutation was very famous at that time.

Morgan wanted to do Hybridisation experiments in animals as Devries did in plants. He chose rats to make his studies on evolution and heredity. He conducted his experiment at Columbia University. He wanted to know how the rat adapt themselves to adverse conditions. But the slow pace of his research made him desperate. At that time the fruit fly or drosophila attracted in attention.

When compared to rats, it was easy to collect and bred drosophila. Male and female differences are very consipicous in them. The drosophila cells carry only two pair of chromosome. That also made Morgan's studies easier. Above all the fruit fly attracted Morgan with its short life span. It needed only twelve days to get a new generation and one pair of fruit flies produce hundreds of offsprings.

Mendel said that the hereditory charcaters are decided by certain factors. Morgan proved Mendel's factor as genes situated on chromosomes found in the nucleus of cells. Morgan prepared a gene map of all the genes of the two pairs of Chromosomes of drosophila. Today Genetics is one of the most advanced branches of Biology. Very elaborate gene maps of several species are available now. When compared to them Morgan's gene map was rather imperfect. But it happened in the second decade of twentieth century and it was a great achievement. Morgan found out the each chromosome of the fruit fly contain at least thousand genes.

Morgan discovered more than hundred mutations in drosophila. Devries argued that single mutations lead to the formation of new species. But Morgan did not agree with it. He found mutations in the traits like colour of eye, colour of body, shape of the wings etc. But this single mutations do not lead to the emergence of a new species. This was morgan's view. He again said that, the variations that Darwin found out might be the result of mutations continueous mutations result in continueous variations and there by the formation of new species. In this way Morgan helped to reach a compromise between theory of mutation Darwin's Natural selection. Now Darwinism combined with Genetic forms. Neo darwinism which is considered as a modern branch of life science.

Single mutations when accumulated effect variation. This is the basic idea of Neo Darwinism. In most cases gene mutation proves to be detrimental to species. Only favourable mutations are selected by Nature and transferred to the next generation.

In 1871 Federic Micher, A German Chemist discovered that genes contain a substance acidic in nature. He named it 'Nuclean.' Later it was known as Deoxyribo Nueclic acid (DNA). At that time scientists were trying to find out the agent who carries the heriditory characters from parents to offsprings. The very question which puzzled Darwin. Some American scientists said that it was the DNA which carried the characters of parents to young ones. But what special structure of the DNA facilitates this transfer was still unknown. 1953 James Watson and Francis Crick, two American scientists found out the chemical structure of DNA. That was an epoch making discovery in Biology. By this discovery they revealed the mystry behind heredity, which the Biologists were searching for since the rediscovery of Mendelism.

DNA molecule resembles a winding staircase. Watson and Crick named it "Double Helix." The two side bars of this staircase are made of sugar and phosphate molecules. Nitrogen bases form the steps of this ladder. There are four types of Nitrogen bases, and they pair in a particular order to form the steps. When gametes are produced the DNA molecules divide into two halves and goes to each gametes. At the time of fertilization the gametes units to form a zygote, each half of DNA in a gametes pairs with the other half and comes back to the original form of Double Helix. From the zygote the whole body cells of a new individual is divided and they carry the replica of the DNA molecule. In this way an offspring gets half of his DNA from father and other half from mother. Like DNA molecules Darwinism and Mendelism fuse here to reveal the mystery of Evolution and Heridity.

The more the Genetics developed the more evidences it brought out to justify Darwinism. A lot of studies were made about variations at both chromosome and gene level. From acellular bacteria to blue whale the structure and replication of DNA molecule are same. This leads to a common ancestor once existed. Richard Dawkins. one of the most famous Geneticist of today states that Natural Selection works at genes level. In a cell the genes compete each other and some genes try to dominate over others. He continues to say that as the preys try to escape from the predators, some genes try to escape from others. The competition among the individuals of the same species points towards the struggle between the genes, Darkins added. Genetic Darwinism is the name he gave to it.

Now even school children knew many things that Darwin didn't know. The fossil collection now we have is beyond his imagination. Several living fossils also have been identified. Still Darwin and Darwinism stands like a light house and pours light on the coming generations also. It will stand there for ever.

12
Newton of Biology

Darwin wrote sixteen books on various areas of Biology. Of these eight books were written after 1859. After the publication of *The origin of species* he wrote only two books on Evolution. The others were related to plants. Some critics had the opinion that Darwin's works on coral reefs and earthworms are more original than *origin of species*. Darwin had made remarkable studies about plant movements. After Darwin, it was Jagadish Chandra Bose, the famous Indian scientist who made significant contributions in this field. After the publication of *The origin of species* Darwin did not continue his research in the field of Evolution. But he never kept himself away from science. Darwin died on 19 April 1882. His last research paper was published just thirteen days before his death. Darwin prepared this paper based on some information he got from the grandfather of Francis Crick. But in the long period of twentythree years after the publication of his famous book, Darwin wrote nothing about his favourite idea, the Natural Selection. He might have thought he had written everything so vividly in his book that there was nothing to be added. Or was it because Darwin was unwilling to discuss the shortcoming of his book.

Still *The origin of species* is considered as Darwin's most significant work. Among Darwin's books it was most widely read and widely discussed. Copernicus broke the shackle that religion and Church put around science. That declaration of independence got perfection through Darwin' theory of evolution. Above a mere scientific principle Darwin's theory was a vision that changed the direction of human thought. Darwin categorically denied the idea that man has a special position in this universe. Owing to Darwin our entire picture of man and his place and role in Nature has been changed. Darwin very clearly stated that man had originated from an ancestor more or less ape- like and to be placed in the same group of exisiting apes. Man cannot be considered as a Lord of other creations and he is only a part of the nature. Man had the same right on this earth as the other species have. Like other species man has also evolved through various stages and his descent took millions of years. This is the lesson that Darwin teaches us through his book and this is the lesson that we have to learn yet. Towards the end of his book Darwin says that in the near future. "Light will be thrown on the origin of man and his history."

One of the branches of tree of Evolution ends in dog and other in Tape worm and the third one in mango tree the fourth branch will have man on its tip. Everyone was transformed through Natural Selection. So how can we argue that one species is greater than the other? Darwin was the first naturalist who proved that like physics and Chemistry Biology also can be explained with the help of certain Natural laws. Till then people resorted to God to explain matters relating to living organisms.

Both Darwin and Wallance introduced a new theory of change to scientific world. That was the gradual change by which new species are formed. Upto then the only changes known to science was chemical change and physical change. The awareness that changes occurs in organic world forced people to approach Biology as a pure science. Today we treat Physics, Chemistry and Biology as three branches of knowledge we are indebted to Darwin for this. Darwin knew nothing about the laws of heredity. About the orgin of life also he was in total ignorance. The hypothesis the life originated from non-living things was already rejected before Darwin's time. Francisco Redy, an Italian doctor proved this in 1688. Louis Pasteur the great French scientist also proved that no living beings originated from non-living objects. Anton Van Leeuwen hook discovered microscope. With the help of his this microscope Leeuwenhook saw several micro organisms. If we trace back Darwin's common ancestor we must reach micro organisms. There we find ourselves in a blind alley. How did the first living organism originate? What was its nature? What was its chemical nature? How did the cellular organisms divide into multicellular plants and cells? Darwin left these questions unanswered. He wrote nothing about the process now we call chemical Evolution. But Darwinism gave scientists confidence that in the near future they would find out the answers to these questions. It happened in 1953 about hundred years after the publication of *The origin of species.*

The synthesis of Amino acid molecule in a laboratory was that great incident. Amino Acids unite to form protein. Protein is the most important constituent of living cell. Questions still remained. How can one distinguish living things from non-living things? What is the difference between them. Darwinists claim that all these questions have answers in Darwin's theory. According to them anything that undergo Evolution through Natural Selection in a living being.

After Darwin Biology got a special position because it is the only branch of science where there is the direct action of Nature? Before other scientists he presented a classic example of research project. It was very accurate and systematic that anybody with a little scientific attitude could not but appreciate. His thesis written in simple language is a marvellous example of scientific writing. After reading *the origin of species* Thomas Henri Huxely, the famous English Naturalist exclaimed "How simple! why couldn't I think it earlier!" Later Huxely, who was a friend of Darwin engaged in the Campaign for Darwinism. It should be remembered that Darwin made such an elaborate study during a period when the various branches of Biology like embryology, Biochemistry, Ecology and Palentology lay in an embryonic stage.

Darwin made Biology to stand upon its own legs without the support of God. Even a staunch advocate of Darwinism would not claim that everything Darwin told was correct. Even Darwin would not say that. But Darwinism had been recognised as an undeniable scientific theory. It fell on the Victorian consciousness like lightening. Darwin used simple language and communicated directly to his readers. It was not easy to raise objections, against it, as Darwin had answers to almost all expected questions.

Alfred Wallace in his book on Darwinism praises Darwin as the Newton of Biology. That is a good comparison. As physics is divided before Newton and after Newton, Biology also can be divide before Darwin and after Darwin. The only difference is that a common man cannot understand Newton's principles without the help of a teacher or interpreter. On the other hand Darwinism allows a direct entry to any layman.

In the first few decades of Twentieth century we find the lustre of Darwinism a little faded because of the fast growth of genetics. Some people even started writing obituaries for Darwinism. But Darwin's theories had a rebirth through Neo Darwinims. From there onwards Darwinism, Genetics and Biochemistry have a peaceful co-existence.

Darwin never worried about the future of his theory. He was sure that his ideas would bring revolutionary changes in the field of Biology. When we understand the hereditary relations between the species it is easy to comprehend their similarities in morphology and the reasons for variations. Between the designing and production of a large machine there is a long history of hard work, repeated trails and unexpected failures. Similarly when we observe a living being the long years of planning variations and selection by Nature come to our mind and it becomes very easy to understand the natural instincts and complicated anatomy, and morphology exhibited by it. We find that there is nothing unintelligible in it and that makes natural science a very interesting subjects. As Darwin prophesied several new branches of studies have been established in the real of natural science. As natural selection works solely by and for the good of each being, all corporeal and mental endowments will tend to progress towards perfection. Human mind also developed through modification and evolution. The immense advance that pshychology made in the twentieth century also tells us that Darwin is always correct.

Darwinism attracted historians social scientists and politicians. It was for the first time a scientist talking about progress. He described species being modified during a long course of descent. In Physics and Chemistry one can make new inventions and bring it to application level without knowing the previous works done in that field. But in the case of evolution no one grasp the essence of this idea without understanding the continuity of developments of organic beings.

The scientists who talked about evolution before Darwin agreed on the presence of a divine hand behind the creation of new species. Both Lamarch and Robert Chambers pointed out that new species were formed from older ones. But they also did not deny the role of a divine hand. None of them but only Darwin told about a common ancestor.

The attitude of the English society was in a transitional stage when Darwins theories came out. The slogans of French Revolution.

liberty, equality and fraternity were fast spreading among the labour class of England. Democrats and social democrats quoted Lamarck when critising church and government. Lamarck had said that the species of lower plant with the action of internal force, will modify themselves to species of higher plane. In the same way the labourers suppressed by the capital force would break their bonds and come out as a new force with new vigour. Darwin's theory that no species is specially created by God and everyone is descended from a common ancestor made them happy and excited.

Darwin brought Biology near to philosophy. The nineteenth century witnessed several inventions. Most of them were related to the field of industry and technical education. They helped the development of industry and capitalist production. So the progressive thinkers placed them at the opposite side of humanity. Darwin's theory was something the capitalists could not exploit. His theory embraces all living organisms from amaeba to blue whale. To study Darwins theory one must not have well equipped laboratory or complicated machinery. Grass and grass hopper, Flowers and butterflies, Fish and frogs ass and horse include the evidence of Darwin's theory. They were everywhere around and very easy to find. This was a rare experience. It was no wonder that people from all walks of life came forward to get a copy *The origin of species.*

We have seen that all the 1250 copies of first edition of the book were sold out in one day. One of who obtained a copy was Friedrich Engles, then living in Manchester. Engels considered Darwin's theory as one of the three important milestones in the road of progress of science.

According to him the law of conservation of energy is the first milestone. By this discovery the natural phenomena like heat, light, electricity and magnetism became no more enigmatic. The law of conservation of Energy demolished the belief that natural phenomena could not be explained using human parameters. It became clear that energy can neither be crated or destroyed but one from the energy can be converted into another. The knowledge that there is only one energy that exists in different forms helped scientists to explain all natural forces.

In 1838 and 1839 Theodar Schwann and M J Shliedon, two German scientists discovered that the body of all animals and plants are made of cells. This is known as the 'cell theory.' They also declared that new cells are formed from existing cells. According to Engels this was a great discovery because it explained the growth of multicellular organisms as cell division in conformation with certain natural laws.

If cell division is the basis of growth in all multicellular organisms including man how do these innumerable variation occur? Since Darwin's theory provides answer to these question Engels considers it as the third great discovery. Darwin established on evolutionary series starting from simple organisms and ending in man. With the help of Darwin's theory Engels found it eash to explain biodiversity in nature and interpret the development of mental powers.

Engles was close friend and political associate of Karl marx. They met 1848 their friendship lasted till marks death in 1883. That was one of the most celebrated and umparalled comradeship in human history. They shared every new idea between them. After started reading Darwin's book Engels wrote to Max. "Darwin by the way whom I am reading now is absolutely splended. Never before has so grandiose an attempt been made to demonstrate historical evolution in nature, and certainly never to such good effect."

After reading Engles handed over the book to marx. After reading on 19 December 1860 Marx wrote to Engels calling it "the book which contains the basis in natural history of our view."

13

Darwin and Karl Marx

Karl Marx migrated is England with family in 1849. Before that he had visited England and the industrial city of Manchester in 1945. Just as Darwin's visit to Galapagos was the major turning point in his life, Marx's visit to Manchester was a major milestone in his life. The variations seen among the Finches of the Galapagos island sowed the seeds of theory of Evolution in Darwin's mind. How it germinated. we have already seen. The suffering of the industrial labourers made Marx to formulates a theory of liberation for all working class of the world.

Marx was shocked to watch the pathetic lives of the improverished labourers. The moral values which are thought as great and holy had no place in their lives. The family relationships were shattered. Marx saw mothers giving opium to their children while they were away in the factories. The girl child was considered as a burden to the family and were got married at an early age. Marx had already developed a political ideology and this scenes of merciless poverty might have persuaded to come to a determination that he must stand with the poor and downtrodden.

Darwin was never an inspiration or a guide to Marx, because

the ideology that changed the destiny of humanity had been already formulated by Marx and Engels years before the publication of Darwin's book. The *communist manifesto* jointly written by Marx and Engels was published in 1848. George Bernardshaw, the famous English writer commented that Marx changed the mind of the word. Marx who changed the mind of the world needed no more changes by reading Darwin. But he thought Darwin's book was most important and suited his purpose as it provided a basis in natural science for the historical class struggle.

Unlike Engels Marx had no deep knowldge in science. In a letter he writes to Engels that he was going to concentrate more on scientific topics. But Marx observed very keenly all advances that contemporary science made. He always showed a scientist's inquistiveness. He never believed in the theory of creation. He paid no attention to theories of evolutions that appeared before Darwin. But Lyell's book, *The basic princples of Geology* fascinated Marx. It was because Lyell rejected the idea that the earth and all the living things on it were created by God.

In a previous chapter we have seen that Darwin also was facinated by Lyell's book. Lyell had a strong influence on Darwin. Lyell found out that earth was subjected to continuous changes. Darwin assumed that if the earth had been changed this change would be reflected on the living organisms also. "Many of the ideas in my book appear to have came from Lyell's Brain" admitted Darwin very generously. But in the begining Lyell was not ready to support Darwin's theory about organic evolution. Later he changed his opinion and insisted Darwin to send the manuscript of *The origin of the species* to the publisher.

In fact the ideas described in Lyell's book is a continuation of the principles put forward by James Hutton, who lived in eighteenth century. Hutton is honoured as the father of modern Geology. Hutton argued that metamorphosis occurs on earth's surface as well as interior. The physical Phenomena like wind, rain, water flow, heat and pressure inside the earth effect such changes. If the earth was like a uadd prepared by a good cook there wouldn't be such changes Hutton believed that this transformation is a continuous process because the influence of heat, pressure wind and water is always there.

Hutton's comment on earth is very famous. "I see no sign of a begining or an end." Rocks and mountains are formed through process lasting for millions of years. Then the earth must be much older than Bishop Light foot calculated. The church raised objections against this theory. After the French Revolution the upperclass in the English society was afraid of new ideas. So Hutton's discoveries were obscured.

When Charles Lyell found out that his owb ideas are very similar to Hutton's, he became a strong supproter of Hutton. Lyell modified Hutton's ideas and acted as its spoke person. Fortunately the political atmosphere in England also was changing. The Britsh throne itself came forward to recognise new ideas. The queen honoured Charles Lyell with knighthood. *The basic principles of Geology'* had twelve editions during his life time.

Marx was familar with Charles Lyell's ideas. So he was not too much excited when he read Darwine book. As said earlier theories of evolution came out before Darwin did not impress Marx. In his view they were mere ideologies. Though some of the naturalists collected evidences relating evolution they did not reveal them for fear of church and clergy. But Darwin put forward his theory of evolution with the support of enough evidences. Nobody could question him. His theory influenced both intelligence and imagination of mankind. No scientific principle had ever done this. But only a few people recognised the social relevence of Darwin's theory at that time. Marx was one among them.

When T H Huxely conducted a service of talks on Darwinism,

Marx himself attended them and persuaded his friends to do the same. Politics, Economics and Social Science were Marx's favourite subjects. All these three disciplines are directly related to humanity. Thanks to Darwin Biology also got a place among them. Nobody can deny that the history of life and development of mind is directly related to humanity. The advance in the field of Anthropology must have strengthened this bond. But unfortunately when Biology advanced and extended to various areas it distanced itself from social science, and now we see them placed in watertight compartments.

The slogans Marx raised for the working class shook the well established principles of capital- labour relation. Darwin eradicated the belief that living organisms are fixed and only God can change them. Darwin succeeded in liberating Natural science from theology. That was why Darwin's theory attracted Marx. He regarded Darwin's theory progressive and an advance over previous theories. When Darwin acted as a corrective force on the then existing belief about living organisms. Marx reoriented the political and economic relations of his time.

All new theories become established by rejecting the older ones. At the same time each new theory is a continuation of the old. Darwin believed that all species undergo change and modifications. Both of them utilized the knowledge about the past of understand the present. Marx also talked about change. Everything would change. So the capitalist system also would change. All capitalist establishment would be eradicated from earth just as the old species became extinct and a new system would take its place. After all both of them tried to make change in the bourgeois order. In 1883 at Marx's funeral Engels said "just as Darwin discovered the law of development of organic nature, so Marx discovered the law of development of human history."

Darwin didn't give Marx new ideas, but he made Marx more optimistic.

In 1873 Marx sent Darwin a copy of the second German Edition of *Capital* on the title page it was written "Mr Charles Darwin on the part of his sincere admirer Karl Marx." Three months later on 1 October 1873 Darwin wrote a formal reply to Marx thanking him for the gift. This is all that we have about the acquaintance of two great men who lived in the same city for more than thirty years. Did they ever meet? Nobody recorded such a meeting.

Did Darwin read Marx's book. Most people believe that as Darwin was not good at German he did not read Marx. After Darwin's death, the book was found among his papers, left most of its pages uncut and made no pencil mark in the margin as was his custom when reading. Another reason Darwin's negligence to Marx's send book was his back of interest in politics. Then why did Marx his book to Darwin? Marx was never a Darwin devotee and disagreed with him in many ways. But he wanted to circulate his ideas among prominent intellectuals in England. Unlike Darwins' book *Capital* had not received any attention in the British Press at that time.

14
Darwin and Man

From 1938, when Darwin was first working out his ideas the political climate of England was changing. Materialism was popular in respectable circles. England was swept by unprecedented political protests and strikes. The bourgeois class feared a revolutionary change.

The materialistic and atheistic idea became very popular among the working class. Art and literature also was changing. The classisicm was replaced by romanticism. In the classic period the stories and poems were written in the language of sourt and the themes were woven around kings and lords. The romatic period saw literary works written in language used by common people and they began tell layman's stories. The working class also began to enjoy literature. The middle class and upper class feared attack from the working class that belonged to the lower stratism of the society. Darwin was never actively involved in politics. He was a member of a wealthy middle class family. Communist and Socialist ideas never attracted him. Darwin firmly believed that all living organisms were originated from a common ancestor. That was an entirely materialistic idea. Darwin knew that all people are equal in the eye of nature. Still he showed no affinity to communist ideology. The reason was his family background.

Charles Darwin was a representative of bourgeois middle class order. J B Foster wrote, Darwin's science was revolutionary, but Darwin the man was not. Not only Darwin almost all his fellow scientists also belonged to this class. Darwin completed his book in 1844. He was not at all doubtful about his ideas. Still he was hesitant to publish it. In fact Darwin did not want to be identified with the radicalists and materialists. His wife Emma Darwin who was very pious also compelled him to hold it back. Did Darwin fear that his collegues would ostracize him? There are enough reason to believe that.

Darwin competed a 270 page book on his theory in 1844. He attached a letter to it asking his wife to publish it after his death. It is unbelievable that Darwin who developed his theory through years of careful study and experimentation wished to keep it as secret. But he had to publish it in 1859. The incidents that led to the publication of *The origin of species* is already given in the fourth chapter.

Charles Darwin who put forward the most materialistic ideas in the feild of Natural Science never met Karl Marx who came with most revolutionary ideas in the field of politics Economics and Sociology. Now you know the reason.

After publishing *The origin of species.* Darwin wrote another book with name *The Descent of Man.* In this book he substantiate the idea that man like all other species has evolved through Natural Selection. According to Darwin the germs of morality and social sense lie in other species also as natural instincts. In man they appear in the most developed state because of Natural Selection. Darwin points out the examples of social life in animal world. These species depend upon each other for food and protection. In the struggle for existence the chances of survival for these species are greater than the species those have no social life. So this social life is always protected through Natural Selection.

When human races are engaged in competition the races with better intelligence and social sense win. Darwin believed nature's evolutionary laws embrace every living organisms including man. The features exhibited by lower species develop into most perfect state in man. Here also Darwin denies the role of a super power. Darwin argued that the characters of an individual is decided by the development of the natural instincts from within. As said earlier these instincts reach their perfection only in man, but their development is very slow. But Marx firmly believed that when the socio-economic conditions changed there would be quick change in human behaviour also. If Darwin had read *capital* he would have taken socio-economic evolution also into consideration along with organic evolution.

In 1859, Marx also published a book by name *A critic of political Economy* which analysed history from a communist point of view. But unlike Darwin's book Marx's book did not attract readers. Darwins book was sold out as hot cake. During his life time none of Marx's book was sold in that manner. It was only after his death his works including *capital* became the Holy scriptures of the working class. Like Darwins *The origin of species* Marx's books also are translated in many languages and had several editions.

As Marx had no permanent income he was always dogged by financial problems. Jenny, his wife who came from a wealthy family was always worried about the poverty her children had to suffer. Jenny wished if some of her husband's books were sold as that of Darwin's and he become famous. This is revealed in the book *Love and Capital* written by Mary Gabriyest.

As stated earlier marx had nothing to be studied from Darwin but he wished Darwinism got wide publicity. He thought Darwins ideas would be a great help in changing the society in the pattern he wanted. When some people called him "The Darwin of social science" he never objected to it. Though disagreed in many ways he had liked Darwin.

Still it is to be remembered that Marx had no blind admiration towards Darwin. But he was not a hostile critic also. Marx sent a copy of *capital* to Darwin. It was not only out of administration as explained earlier. He sent a copy of his book to Herbert Spencer also. Marx and Engels always opposed Spencer's idea, especially in the feild of Economics.

Marx liked Darwin's idea that all species move to a higher plane through natural selection. He believed history also was moving towards a higher plane to progress and prospertiy. Marx had a clear vision about the life of the working class and the goal they had to achieve. Darwin writes that nature has no such goal. He views road from the distant past and towards eternal future. Through this long road species move very slowly towards progress and perfection Marx who always dreamed the liberation of the working class was not ready for such a long wait. The way the capitalist system expoited the labourers hurt Marx very much. The working class was deprived of all facilities. The exploiters amassed large amount of wealth and the labourers became poorer and poorer.

How can they wait long thinking that time will change everything very slowly. Marx dreamed of a socialist revolution through which the organised working class could control the methods of production and distribution. Only human being are able to see such dreams.

Marx did not like the way Darwin applied the same principles to both man and other living beings. Social life and intelligence distinguish man from others. Another point that Marx disagreed with Darwin was the over importance he gave to Malthus. Marx found Malthus assumption that his law of overpopulation as an eternal law was an error. Marx believed that each mode of production had its own distinct population laws. He said that an abstract law of population existed only for plants and animals. Engels said that struggle for existence occurs only among plants and animals of lower category. And that also at certain stages of development only. According to Marx everybody competing against every body is bourgeois economic theory. Darwin took this theory along with Malthusian population theory and placed in the organic world. Both Marx and Engels disagreed with it. They argued that geological changes would lead to organic evolution without the aid of Malthuscianism.

15
And miles to Go

Darwinism helped to remove ignorance and misunderstandings about life. But some people used Darwinism intentionally to inculcate some false beliefs in Capitalistic society. This was based on struggle for existence and survival of the fittest. Darwin got these ideas from Malthus. In his essay Malthus chiefly talked about population. Resources will not increase at the rate of population. Here arises competition and in this struggle the poor people will be eliminated. Increased food production and better social security methods are its remedies. Malthus did not believe in such measures. Don't you remember his suggestion that the poor should be shipped away to some distant colonies? Communism declares that everyone has the right to lead a descent life. As the advocates of communism and socialism how can Marx and Engels agree with Malthus?

Malthusian principle was placed in nature by Darwin. When a competition takes place in nature only better adapted species will survive and others perish without bringing forth offsprings. Some people tried to contain Darwinism into political and economic situations of England. In the struggle for existence only with better modifications could survive. In a society when such struggle came into being, only rich people would survive, because they would have the facilities to survive adverse situations like epidemic, fanine and climate changes. Herbert Spencer the famous philosopher had no hesitation to say that Natural Selection would help to create a better English society, but only if it was free to operate so that unfit will be eliminated. For that We wanted put an end to public education, compulsory Vaccination, free libraries, workplace safety, laws and charitable support for the poor what a supreme idea!

Supporters of capitalism named it as social Darwinism and began to propagate it. What Darwin put forth as the laws of Nature was again interpreted as laws of God. Millionaires claimed that the growth of large business was merely a survival of the fittest. In this situation Marx and Engels came forward criticising Darwin.

Marx and Engels always talked about classwar. The Goal of classwar is to bring all modes of production and distribution under the control of working class. It can be attained only through continuous mass movements. A capitalist society will never accept a war between the 'Haves' and 'Have nots' Before the apperance of Darwin the spokerspersons of capitalism spoke about co-operation and reconciliation. Suddenly they began to tell about struggle for existence and survival of the fittest. Engels ridiculesr this social Darwinians calling them bad scientists, bad philosophers and bad economists.

In his last book, *The Dialects of Nature*. Engels writes "The present Darwinians earlier talked about co-operation in the living world. Plants provide food and oxygen to the animals and animals give nutrition to plants. But when Darwinism gained popularity they began to talk about struggle and competition." In Engel's opinion both these views are onesided. The processes of living world comprise of competition and co-operation. Nature can't exist only with struggles.

Well developed brain, empowered mind and social and cultural life differentiate man from other living organisms. So like other living being man need not have to engage in compitetion with others. Man can produce things he wants and he can control the production in the nature also. Animals can collect food but man can produce. The productivity of the world is determined by men, not by animals. So the laws governing the life of plants and animals cannot be applied in the case of mankind.

The changes in the enviornment make changes in the living beings. But the only species that can change the environment and there by influences the life of other species is man. In the origin of species Darwin vividly describes how men make use of the variation in domestic animals and birds to select the betters varieties. We can criticise Darwin for not taking into consideration the socio-economic relations among men. He might have thought as a Naturalist that was not his duty. Darwin was interested in the variations seen in men as a species. Marx wanted to change the entire social structure.

Marx raised several critisims against Darwinism. But he never rejected Darwin's principles. No real communist can reject or neglect Darwinism. As Paul Hayer said a Biologist can be a Darwinist without learning Marxism, but no one can be a Marxist without recognising Darwinism.

Darwin died 1882. Next year Marx also passed away. But these two names will remain forever in the history of humanity. When Genetics began to advance, there was a clamour that Darwinism had died. But we saw that Darwinism had a rebirth through Neo Darwinism. At the onset of globalisation, in the first half of eighties the corporates competed in making the whole world their market. The capitalism was trying to come back in different forms. A new phase of colonisation is seen here without establishing colonies and ruling distant lands the corporates were able to increase their profit compete each other in increasing capital. Exploitation gained new pace. People began to question the relevence of Marx. All the world was becoming a single market. Marx wanted to narrow the gap between the bourgeois and proliterians But in the age of globalisation everybody is exploiting and every one is being exploited. But in the last decade we saw protests raising everywhere especially in third world against exploitation of corporates. The world is rediscovering that 'Marx is right.'

Evolution will take place as long as there is life on earth. So Darwinism is relevent for ever. A new species will not appear abruptly before our eyes one day becasue all these species are formed by natural selection through millions of years. A man's life span is so small when compared to that long period. Can man witness the appearance of a new species? Some scientists are trying it. Two Scientists- Rose mary Grant and Peter Grant- have been living in Galapagos islands Since 1873 observing Darwin's finches. They are watching the microvariations happening to them and how these variation are accumulating to become a notable change. They have claimed that they were able to see Finches with large beaks among birds with small beaks. We can hope that in the near future we will get reports from Naturalists who witnessed Evolution before their eyes.

Darwin said that species evolved through natural selection would be better equiped for adaptation than their predecessors. When we look around we become doubtful about it. For the vertebrates the most comfortable posture is on four legs. But man who occupies the top most step of evolutionary ladder moves on two legs. No other animal except man suffers back pain. The optic, auditory and- factory organs are sharper in most other species than human beings -Why is it so! It may be lost due to continuous disuse because our modern life demands no sharp sight, hearing or scenting as our predecessors. Our ancestors who lived in dense forests needed sharp sense organs in order to get food and escape from enemies. This is the same process as the cave dwellers lost their eyesight.

After the discovery of computer chips the habit of memorising has become weaker and weaker. Even a small mobile phone can store a lot of data which we had learned by heart earlier. To the next generation sharp memory will not be a necessary quality. At the same time human brain will evolve itself into new wonderful capacities. This also is a Natural Selection Engels says that any advance in an organic evolution is a reuding also.

Darwin ends his book with these words.

> It is interesting to contemplate a tangled bank, clothed with many plants of many kinds, with birds singing on the bushes with various insects flitting about and with worms crawling through the damp earth, and so reflect that these elaborately constructed forms. so different from each other and dependent upon each other, in so complex a manner, have all been produced by laws acting around us. These laws taken in the largest sense being growth with reproduction, inheritance and variability from the indirect and direct action of conditions of life and from use and disuse. A ratio of increase so high as to lead to a struggle for life and as a consequence of Natural Selection entailing Divergence of character and Extinction of less improved varieties. Thus from the war of nature, from famine and death the most exalted object which we are capable of conceiving namely the production of higher animals, directly follows. There is grandeur in this view of life, with its several powers having been originally breathed by creator into a few forms or into one; and that while this planet has gone cycling on according to the fixed law of gravity from so simple a beginning endless forms most beautiful and most wonderful have been and are being evolved."

Man is still in search of that first throb life Darwin mentioned.